About the Author

Derek Smith has lived most of his life in the East End of London. He was writer-in-residence for Soapbox Theatre in Newham, and was also a founder of Page One bookshop in Stratford. He has had plays produced for radio, television and the stage. His published works include nine children's books, three of which were published by Faber; a collection of short stories for adults, *Strikers of Hanbury Street*; a poetry anthology, *Catching Up*; and *Hell's Chimney*, a fantasy novel. For many years, he has run story-writing workshops in schools, and is a tutor in creative writing at the Mary Ward Centre in Bloomsbury.

Other Books by Derek Smith

Hell's Chimney
Strikers of Hanbury Street (short stories)
Catching Up (poetry)

Children's Books
Hard Cash
Half a Bike
Frances Fairweather Demon Striker!
Fast Food
The Good Wolf
Baker's Boy
Jack's Bus
The Magical World of Lucy-Anne
Lucy-Anne's Changing Ways

The Prince's Shadow

Derek Smith

Earlham Books

Published 2013 Earlham Books, London
Cover image and book design by Lia Rees

This book is printed mainly in **Garamond** font. The title,
chapter headings and page numbers are in **Kingthings Petrock**.

ISBN: 978-0-9565801-4-6

Chapter 1

Cadd was in the oven, lying flat on his back, with his head against the rear wall. The shelves had been taken out, and the brick ceiling curved over him like a sarcophagus. In his right hand was a scrubbing brush with which he was vigorously scrubbing, and grimacing as it dripped onto his face. A fleck of paint chipped out, revealing the brick underneath. He cursed and picked up the fleck; it was the size of his thumbnail, shaped like a man's head with a very pointed chin and a rounded nose. He wondered how many layers of whitewash had gone into it. Back to his grandfather's time and beyond, perhaps.

His back was stiff, he was hungry too but there'd be no eating until dark. A drink of water would hold back the pangs. Cadd inched his way out of the oven, feet first, carrying the wooden bucket on his stomach. The difficult bit was when he was half in and half out, and his feet searched for the floor with his back arched like a bow.

'Why do you always have to come out like that?' said his father in annoyance, taking the bucket off Cadd's stomach, allowing the young man to ease his chest and head through the oven door. For a second or two, after he had found the ground, he felt dizzy and tottered on his feet. It was the sudden movement and the lack of food.

'Can I change the water?' he said as he steadied himself.

His father looked into the bucket. The water was scummy and crusted.

'Carry on with that,' he said. 'We've only half a barrel left.'

The boy nodded. His father's white apron was soaked from where he'd been scrubbing the walls. His clothes hung on him; he'd lost a lot of weight in the past weeks.

Until these days Cadd had known his father as chubby, as befits a baker. While he wasn't exactly thin yet, it was the grey pallor of his skin that would make you wonder about the quality of his bread.

Jel, his big brother, was scrubbing the shelves standing on a stool. He was sighing in annoyance and splashing water. Cadd knew his father was deliberately ignoring Jel. He too had the same grey colour, as did his mother who was banging about in the scullery. It was a family trait; Cadd wasn't left out. Father called it bad bread shadow.

'When's the flour coming?' Cadd asked.

'Don't ask stupid questions,' his father snapped and clipped him about the head. It didn't hurt, but the young man scowled. 'You're as bad as that lot,' shouted his father, indicating the window and the faces pressing in.

'I should have joined the bloody army,' exclaimed Jel, jumping off his stool. 'Instead of washing and cleaning things which are clean already.'

'Do you think they don't wash and clean in the army?' said his father sourly.

'I'm hungry and I'm fed up,' said Jel throwing his brush into his bucket with a splash.

'You can't be both,' said Cadd.

'Shut up, Pipsqueak.'

Mother came out of the scullery in a rush. Her hands were white, bubbly and rippled. Her greying hair was hanging lank over her shoulders. 'That's every pot, pan, tin, spoon, whisk, ladle, cup and bowl done,' she said with the biggest sigh. 'When's the flour coming?'

Father clapped his hands to his head. 'Don't keep asking! I go every day to the miller. He says soon. He says we're on the list. I ask him how soon is soon. He says soon as they say. I say soon we'll be dead. He says the flour might come first or – it might not.' Father stopped, gritted his fists, closed his eyes and stood as if turned to stone by the forbidden question. His wife came behind, and put an arm round his shoulder. She wiped her nose with the back of her hand and nodded to her sons.

'Soon,' she said weakly.

'Never,' shouted Jel. 'I've had enough.'

He went to the shop door and ripped it open. Sunlight made a path to the big, wooden, scrubbed table and over it, and poked into the entrance of the oven, where it gave up.

Jel stood in the doorway.

'Go home!' he yelled to the crowd. 'We have no flour. The oven is cold. We are not getting any flour. Don't waste your time here!'

His father pushed his tall son out of the way. 'I'm sorry,' he shouted. Cadd could just see past him, the line running down to the corner, the same deep sunk pallid faces. 'I want to bake you all bread...' his father went on.

And then his father sank to his knees. His hands covered his face as if he was ashamed before them. What does a baker do if he doesn't bake? his father had said yesterday. From the age of ten his father had got up in the dark, mixing the dough, pounding the dough, letting it rise, filling the tins, baking... That's all he'd ever done.

The crowd did not know the answer either. They waited and hoped without hope. The baker had always baked. Every morning early the smoke would waft from the oven chimney, and a little later, floating out of the shop window, would come the smell of yeast and hot bread.

His mother had gone outside and was standing over his father. Cadd sat on a stool. No one was moving out front. They were waiting for the miller. And the miller was waiting for...? Cadd sighed. There was a little bread in the larder he knew. The family couldn't eat it in daylight, not with everyone watching, suspecting the baker had kept some back. Which he had.

Could he sneak a bit now, with everyone out front? They'd beat him black and blue if they caught him – but he was so hungry...

It was then they came.

Not the miller with flour. That would have been too soon. But the soldiers.

Chapter 2

There were five of them. Four carried the ceremonial spears of the King's guard over their shoulders; the other, the captain, had a short sword at his belt. They wore the traditional red uniform, with its ornate jacket, short bunched trousers over white leggings, and red soft cap with yellow piping.

The captain looked about him in disapproval at the queue, then at the shop and the people before it.

'Anyone here Nat the master baker?' he said.

Mother's hand went to her mouth in alarm. And the crowd as one looked to the baker.

'I am,' said Father.

The crowd edged in eagerly. What had the baker been caught for? They suspected as much.

The captain faced Father, looked him up and down. 'You are the fourth son of your father, Jeb, also a master baker?'

'I am,' said Father, scratching his neck. 'Is there anything wrong?' he added timidly.

The captain ignored him. 'You have four sons?' he enquired.

'I do,' said Father. 'The two eldest are in the army with General Hal. That's Jel, my third.' He pointed him out and Jel smiled weakly. 'And my youngest is in the shop.'

'Get him outside,' ordered the captain.

Father nodded rapidly and swallowed.

'Cadd!' he shouted, his voice trembling. 'Come out here at once.'

Cadd quickly closed the larder door. He brushed the crumbs around his mouth and off his clothing. And chewed as quickly as possible the lump of hard bread. He began to walk slowly, gulping as he came, licking his gums and poking with his fingernail to remove the remnants stuck in his teeth.

'At once!' shouted his father, the alarm in his voice panicking Cadd.

He rushed out of the shop, blinking in the sunlight, wondering at all this urgency, hoping it wasn't trouble. The four red guards were in a line, their spears all at the same angle. The captain stood by his father. Mother's lip was trembling. Jel caught his eye and shrugged – meaning what? The crowd stared.

Cadd's knees began to shake. This couldn't be good.

'Number four?' said the captain.

'Yes,' said Father.

'No daughters?'

Father shook his head.

'You have to come with me, boy.'

Cadd looked to his mother and father in puzzlement. 'Do I?' he said barely audibly.

'He's only a youngster. Why must he go?' said Father.

'Because he has to,' said the captain. 'That's why.'

'Is it bad?' said Father.

The captain spread his hands. 'Don't ask me, because I don't know. I'm just here to collect him.'

'I would like to accompany you. If I may,' said Father.

The captain shook his head. He pointed at Cadd with his forefinger. 'Him. Alone.'

Father looked about wildly as if help might come out of the crowd, or even through the house walls. He was just a baker. What did he know of the ways of the law?

Mother half curtseyed and said, 'Where will you take him, sir?'

The captain considered whether to ignore the woman, then decided respect should be encouraged. 'The castle,' he said. 'I hand him over to the Proctor.'

'When will he come back, sir?'

The captain shrugged. 'Could be a couple of hours.' He eyed the crowd in disdain. Not a lot of respect there. Some of them shuffled closer, so he spoke even more quietly. 'Could be never.'

And in that – the captain was right.

Chapter 3

The captain walked in front. Cadd, with guards on either side, was two paces behind. And two further paces behind them were the other guards. They did not hold him, nor did they speak to him. He was being escorted – and whoever had given them orders had not said why. In such cases the captain knew it was best to be careful. All this might simply be a prelude to arrest – in which case the party was scum and could be treated as such. But it might be the precursor to a knighthood; in such cases correctness and good manners paid off. Not that the latter seemed likely, but stranger things had happened. And what with all that fourth son of a master baker stuff... It would be best to just get him there in one piece and hand over.

They were walking down the middle of the high street. All the food shops on either side were shut. There were no stalls out. Beggars lay or sat in the gutter, hands permanently out, eyes sunken in bony faces, some evidently close to death. A woman sitting on the kerb with a shawl over her head had two infants by her. All three held out their hands but seemed to see nothing and no longer bothered to ask. Cadd hated coming this way. His family ate better than some but had nothing to spare. And if they had – what would all these beggars do with the crust his family could spare?

He stared straight ahead, not bothering to ask anything, realising that the soldiers knew little, and would tell him even less. Besides, spears quell a restless tongue. They had allowed him to remove his overalls at the shop, which he gave to his mother. She'd kissed him and told him to be good, just answer their questions and don't talk back. A few heads turned as he came by. He obviously wasn't a prince to be so escorted, but why then wasn't he in chains? It would be something to talk about, he thought, and it wasn't often he was anybody that people talked about. He knew something was going to happen. Maybe he wouldn't spend his life cleaning ovens. Well, he'd prayed to get out of the bakery, but still couldn't evade a shiver, half of fear and half a thrill in the unexpected.

The castle wasn't far ahead; its towers and walls could be seen over the rooftops. He'd never been inside. Not properly, that is. He'd crossed the drawbridge with his father to drop off bread at the guardhouse when for some reason they'd had a shortage. And just seen into the courtyard, but the main buildings... well, they weren't for bakers' sons. Or they hadn't been so far.

A fireball shot over their heads, arched over the road and dropped a few streets to their right. It had obviously come over the walls, fired from some sort of ballista, and a minute or so later came another. From around the streets, he could hear the bells of the fire wagons. It was imperative that they put them out. Most of the town was wood.

Chapter 4

They crossed the drawbridge and stopped at the guardhouse at its end. The captain went inside. The four guards maintained their places – and Cadd stood with them, waiting. A few minutes later the captain came out with a stool. He offered it to Cadd, who sat down outside the guardhouse door. Two soldiers were dismissed and went into the guardhouse. Another was sent off to the main building. He handed his spear to the captain and crossed the courtyard, not a guard anymore but a messenger. The fourth guard stood alongside Cadd. He was the remnant. The captain had gone, done his bit, and was about to hand Cadd on.

Cadd watched what he could he see of the courtyard. A woman was drawing water from the well. First one bucket and then another. He guessed she was from the kitchen. He wondered about the food here. How hard did the shortages bite in the castle? Did the King still eat well? His own family hadn't had meat for months. If they ate it here, it would have to be bacon or salt pork, preserves. There was a regular clanging he couldn't see, probably a blacksmith. Two men were taking casks from a wagon and handing them down to someone in a cellar. The black and white horse was drinking from a bucket. The animal was thin, the skin stretched tight against its ribs.

The guard-messenger came out of the main building, followed by a smart man in a green uniform with gold braid. They crossed the courtyard, the soldier went into the guardhouse and the smart man bent down to Cadd on his stool.

He said, 'I'd be obliged if you would accompany me, master Cadd.'

The 'master' threw him. He wasn't often called that, but the man didn't seem to be joking. Cadd rose and the man walked by his side and they crossed the courtyard together. Cadd thought, he must be important. All that gold in his uniform, and he is going straight into the castle. That surely indicates high rank.

The man said, 'I trust the soldiers were correct in their treatment.'

'I've no complaints,' said Cadd.

Midway across, he could see the blacksmith now, sparks flying as he hit a red-hot piece of metal with a large hammer.

Cadd thought, my father has never been so far. Simply to the guard house, so already he was exceeding him, and each further step took him away from the baker and towards the grandeur of their rulers. They were heading for a wide door, flanked by two guards. His escort ignored the soldiers and walked straight through. After a short vestibule they climbed wide stone steps to a hallway, then began to cross the hallway where tables were being laid, reminding Cadd how hungry he was.

'Excuse me,' he said, a little surprised at his own boldness. 'Can I have some food?'

The man stopped. Cadd halted and wondered whether his mother would judge this as rudeness.

'When did you last eat?'

'Yesterday, sir.' A slight lie, he'd had a nibble just before he'd been taken, but that hardly counted.

'Stay here.'

The man crossed the hall quickly, and went into a room with a wide open door where steam issued. He returned shortly with a thick slice of bread and a cup of beer. He sat Cadd on a chair.

'Eat quickly, please. They are waiting for you.'

The bread was fresh and not adulterated like his father's. The butter on it was heaven. He would have loved to have eaten it slowly, savouring every bite, but the man was impatient, tapping his toe on the floor. Reluctantly he gulped the bread. The beer was good too, not vinegary or flat, and smelt strongly of hops.

Leaving his empty cup on the table, they continued.

They walked along a flagstoned corridor. It curved round slowly, an inner circle within the round building. On one side were high windows filtering in shafts of light, on the other, widely spaced doors. And just as equally spaced were guards in castle uniform, holding spears at their sides.

'How many rooms has the King?' asked Cadd quietly.

'The King owns every room in the Kingdom,' said the man.

This wasn't the answer to Cadd's question, but he thought it would be impolite to rephrase it. Instead he said:

'Have I done something wrong?'

They were walking quite rapidly, their heels ringing on the stones.

'Have you?' said the man.

Cadd was having a little trouble keeping up with the man, and was half running.

'Nothing worse than usual,' he managed to say.

'Don't worry – unless it's treason,' said the man. 'Then worry a lot.'

'I don't know what treason is,' said the younger man.

The man stopped abruptly, and Cadd shot past him before he halted. The man caught him up and tapped him on the chest, looking deep into his eyes.

'Have you been dealing with the enemy?' he said.

'No,' said Cadd fearfully. He'd never ever met any of the enemy.

'Have you been speaking against the King?'

Oh heavens, he wondered. A word or two in the shop, in the privacy of the family, what with all the shortages and fires... Surely he hadn't been overheard?

'No,' he said.

'A loose tongue often ends in a severed head,' said the man.

They were outside a door; this was double the width of most of the others, and guards stood on either side.

'Remember to say Your Majesty,' said the man, tapping out his advice with his forefinger. 'Please and thank you of course. Don't interrupt. If you must disagree – though it's not a good idea – but if you really must then begin: with the greatest respect, Your Majesty – but frankly I wouldn't. Don't forget to bow as you go in and when you leave. And walk backwards of course. Don't fiddle with your fingers or suck your thumb. Answer when requested, and remember you are nothing here. I don't know why they want to see you, but don't bring shame on your family by discourtesy...'

Cadd nodded and nodded as the man went on and on. His knees shook, he'd have trouble saying a word... Perhaps he'd be better off as a baker. What on earth was he doing here?

The man rapped on the door. A single, very polite knock.

A servant in livery came to the door.

'The baker's son,' said the man.

The servant nodded.

The man turned to Cadd. 'Remember my advice,' he said.

And to Cadd's surprise the man strode off down the corridor.

The servant standing at the door wore the same green livery as the man who had just gone, but it had even more

gold piping and extra gold buttons. Cadd knew he had a lot
to learn.

'Come in,' said the servant.

Chapter 5

The room was large with blue draperies hanging from the walls. If there was a window it was hidden by them, and the room lit instead by a number of candles, standing on various chests and tables. There was a carpet in the centre and a wide canopied bed to one side, with the curtains drawn aside. The servant stood by the door, even with all his piping away from the action; this was centred on the bed, where lay an old lady propped up on pillows. By her bedside was a small table covered in bottles and small boxes, some of which were open revealing unguents and powders, filling the room with a thick sweetish smell. Two men stood by the bed, one fat – reminding Cadd of his thoughts about castle food, the other tall and thin, suggesting an alternative answer.

The tall man said, 'Come here, young man.'

Cadd walked to within three paces of the bed and stood to attention.

'Closer,' said the woman in the bed, her voice thick and rasping.

Cadd took a step forward.

'Closer,' she snapped.

Cadd went at once to the bedside.

The old woman gripped his wrist. Her fingers were long and bony, as pale as chicken flesh. Her face was gaunt, her pallid blue eyes deep-sunk. Her lank, long hair was utterly white and the spittle gurgled in her throat as she struggled to breathe.

'Are you the fourth son… of a fourth son… of a master baker?'

'Yes,' nodded Cadd in a frightened whisper.

'Speak up, I can't hear,' rasped the old woman.

'I am, Your Majesty,' he said.

The fat man laughed. The thin man smiled and said, 'I think some introductions are due.'

The old woman scowled. She stuck her fingers in a powder at her bedside table, pulled them out dust-covered, and sucked them eagerly.

'I am the Royal Chancellor,' said the thin man. He wore a black cloak tied at the neck and a soft red hat. A gold chain hung in a half-circle over his white shirt.

'Pleased to meet you, sir,' said Cadd with a bow, hoping that was the right form for a Royal Chancellor.

'And this is His Majesty the King,' went on the thin man, indicating the fat man.

This overwhelmed Cadd. He had already given a bow to the Chancellor. What more was due to a King? He did not know what to do and simply stared.

The King did not look that kingly. He wore no crown. He did wear a gold chain, but that was half hidden in his red cloak under which were layers of embroidered waistcoat. The King's face was as plump as a bulldog's, his jowls loose and floppy. He wore a soft blue hat, cut into thin slices with gold piping like a pie.

'It is customary to kneel,' said the Chancellor.

Cadd at once kneeled and bowed his head. 'Pleased to meet you, Your Majesty.'

The King did not reply.

'And this is Benna,' went on the Chancellor. 'About whom doubtless you have heard.'

He had. Cadd lifted his head. How long would this go on, the introductions? Must he bow and Your Majesty before every single word? Just in case, he put his head down once more so as not to offend.

'Pleased to meet you, Your...' Then stopped. What do you call the Royal Sorceress?

'Benna will do,' said the old lady. 'I don't go in for titles. Well, I did once but got bored with them… In your great-grandfather's time.'

The King nodded.

Cadd was still on his knees looking at the carpet. Benna was said to be 250 years old; some said 500. He had once heard someone say a thousand. It would be impolite to ask her, now he had the opportunity.

'You may stand up,' said the Chancellor.

Cadd stood and raised his head from the totally subservient position a little. He decided to look at stomachs. It was a rule he knew – never catch the eyes of your betters. Also, remembering the advice given at the door, he held his hands together behind his back so he wouldn't be seen to fiddle.

'Come closer,' said the old lady. 'You speak quietly.'

When he was within reach, she gripped him by the wrist again and held him to the bedside.

'Why him?' said the King to the old woman.

'It is foretold,' said Benna, staring at Cadd and making him look away. 'The fourth son of a fourth son of a master baker. It is he and only he who will get through the siege.'

'You know the danger your country's in, boy?' said the Chancellor.

'Yes sir.'

'This town will fall in weeks unless we get help. And then that will be the end of us. The King of Larken will sweep through the Kingdom murdering and enslaving…'

'You must bring help, boy,' said Benna.

'What must I do?' He dropped all address, realising he was important. Or at least they thought he was, which is perhaps the same thing.

'Get a message to General Hal,' said the King. 'He is off fighting in Witland which wasn't the best of decisions, all considered. But I was persuaded...' He sighed deeply, pressing his hands over his rotund belly. 'And the King of Larken saw his chance...' He waved his fat hands helplessly. 'And here we are, surrounded and hungry.'

Cadd didn't think he looked hungry, but of course did not say so. It was so hard not to look at anyone. His eyes rested on the King for an instant, then on the old lady, who terrified them away and onto the rumpled bedclothes.

'Let's not bother the boy with too much detail,' said the Chancellor. Cadd wondered whether he thought him stupid, or so lowly as to not be worth the time. Or both.

The Chancellor took a sealed paper off a table. 'You must get this message to General Hal.'

'You must insist he come at once,' said the King.

Cadd was bewildered. He, insist a General should come at once? A baker's son, fourth son of a fourth son or not. How he had risen in a few minutes! On equal footings with Generals.

'Where is he?' he asked. 'The General,' he added, in case they might have lost the thread.

The King and Chancellor looked at each other.

'We don't know,' said the Chancellor hesitantly, then added more brightly, 'but it shouldn't be difficult to find an army. Should it?'

'No, sir,' said Cadd, as if he were always in the habit of finding lost armies.

'You will be rewarded,' said the King.

Cadd considered this. Rewards were never for nothing.

'Might I not be killed?' he said.

'No,' said Benna and stuck her nails into his wrist. 'It is foretold. The fourth son of a fourth son of a master baker will get through the siege. How many times do I have to tell you?' She was shifting about the bottles and powders by her bedside with the skeletal fingers of her free hand. 'Ah!' She took up a small brown bottle and gave it a good shake. She pulled off the cork with a pop – and sniffed at the contents. 'Yes, that's the one.' She held out the bottle to Cadd. 'Drink it.'

Cadd took it. He grimaced at the acrid smell and hesitated.

'Drink it, boy.'

Cadd shuddered. He looked to them all. They were watching and waiting. He took a deep breath and threw it down his throat.

And at once coughed and spluttered as the liquid exploded within him. His throat was burning, and as it flowed downwards, his gullet and his stomach too. Orange and yellow fire erupted in his eyes and he screamed at the needles sunk into his chest. His limbs strained to fly off like arrows from a battlement, his skull to open and his brain be launched free like a rock from a ballista.

He could not breathe, could not think, words were gone, the room was gone... He was fire and smoke. He was splashing molten metal.

And then it subsided. The fires cooled, the needles were pulled out of his flesh, his limbs came back to his sockets, and his skull shut in his brain. He opened his eyes to find himself lying flat out on the carpet. The King and Chancellor were standing over him, looking down in some concern. The Sorceress was gazing over the side of her bed.

'Stronger than I thought,' she mused.

Cadd could not reply, nor move a limb.

'It will enable you to breathe under water, boy,' she said and smiled at him from a nearly toothless mouth, almost motherly. 'You must cross the river, you know, to get through the lines. In half an hour your limbs will respond again. Don't worry.' She stretched painfully and groaned, trying to scratch her back. To the servant at the door, she exclaimed, 'Plump me up.'

He at once came over and plumped her cushions. At the same time, Cadd noted the King and Chancellor were leaving. He was unable to bow or kneel or give the correct address for when one is leaving the company of the King and his Chancellor. But they didn't seem to mind.

Chapter 6

The night was dark and moonless. The letter was in a sealskin pouch tied to his belt. He wore black clothing: shirt, leggings, shoes. His face and hands had been wiped over with a greasy mixture of goose fat and soot.

A soldier was with him on the wall battlements. He could barely see him in the gloom, but that was all the better, considering what he must do. They spoke in whispers.

'Take your line from the fires,' the soldier said. And he might have been pointing. Or not.

Beyond the wall, out of arrowshot, were the campfires of the enemy. Here and there at roughly equal intervals. He must get beyond them to the river, which he couldn't see at all. Once across, there was another enemy encampment. Through that – and then find General Hal.

Wherever he was.

The rope was thick and rough in his hands and smelled of pitch. One end was tied to an iron ring attached to the battlement wall, the other hung down over the wall.

'Now,' said the soldier. 'And silent as the grave.'

He put a hand on Cadd's shoulder.

'Best of luck, boy.'

'Thank you,' he whispered.

He stepped onto the crenellation, the rope tight in his hands. He knelt down, whispered to himself – *this is it* – and lowered himself over the wall. Walk down the wall, the soldier had said. Cadd kept his feet to the wall as well as he could, leaning outwards, and hand over hand let himself down. It was difficult, he found, to co-ordinate hands and feet. He lost the wall and swung back and forth like a pendulum. He twisted his legs round the rope and lowered himself that way a while. Then his feet found the wall again, and let him walk down it once more, slower this time. That seemed to be the trick; it was speed that had set him swinging. Cadd was unable to see the ground. He hoped the enemy wasn't there, waiting for one of the besieged to drop into their arms.

This was such hot work.

It had taken a while for him to recover from the witch's potion. He'd panicked at one point, thinking he could be stuck this way, prone and helpless on the carpet like a beetle on its back. But motion eased back into his limbs and body. Then he was taken away to be fed. A large meal which had the soldier watching him licking his lips. Then off to a small room to rest, as there were several hours before nightfall. It seemed an endless time, thinking and rethinking all they had told him. Dreams of glory, dreams of death.

The soldier had come, dressed him and blacked him up. Before going up to the battlements, he talked him through getting down the wall and what he might encounter on the way. The soldier was surprised at their choice, but Benna must be respected, he said. There was little enough to save them. No one had yet got through enemy lines. And they must grasp at the smallest straw.

Cadd touched ground. He took a number of deep breaths and felt the pouch was still in place. He pulled at the rope three times, the agreed signal. And instantly he felt it being pulled back up. There – it had gone.

And he must go on. There was no way but forward now.

He lowered himself to a crouch, and began to edge through the trampled grass and mud. He had picked out a rough line through the fires. Slowly, he must go, making no sound to disturb their guard. It had been hot work coming down the wall, but he was cold now. This wasn't the weather for creeping, but creeping was the only way.

There were fires perhaps forty feet to either side. The grass, trampled flat, offered no cover. There were a few tents that assisted, but he must go slow – and hope. Voices stilled him. He could not see them which meant, surely, they could not see him.

It was all very well the witch saying it was foretold: he would get through the lines. Was she always right? She didn't look so healthy herself. All those pots and bottles by her bedside. And that wheeze; she could die any minute. And if she couldn't cure herself – then why believe her prophecy? If she was so magic why couldn't she fly herself to General Hal? Or send a familiar – a cat, a bird. All that fourth son of a fourth son stuff... Why should that have any meaning for anyone?

Suddenly it came to him. He was crawling, mud-covered – the blacking had been superfluous. Fires were on either side and ahead. He was in the midst of them. A shadow with a spear passed a fire then disappeared in the gloom. And then a memory. His mother had said there was a little boy who had died before he was born. Only four months old. What was his name? But never mind names... It meant he wasn't the fourth. He was the fifth son, so even if the witch was right – he was the wrong man!

Fear flooded him. No help from magic, even if there was magic. It had been a hope. He wanted to go back to the wall. *Please let down the rope.* Find the gates, hammer on them. *Let me in, for heaven's sake let me in. I'm the wrong one!*

He lay still, his heart beating in his ears. There was no way back. He could not climb the wall. No one would let down the rope. Or open the gates. And when the dawn came – he would be in the open – and the clearest of targets for the enemy.

Darkness was his only helper.

The enemy might have fires but they carried no torches, or they could be shot at from the battlements. *Darkness – save me.* He crawled on, inching forward. Death lay in every direction. Backwards, forwards, to the side. He had no friend but one.

Footsteps squelched in the grass. He lay flat out, as muddy as the mud he lay in. There were hushed voices, a laugh, a rattle of metal. Squelching feet, like a conversation in some muddy tongue. They came close and stopped. How far – he dared not look. How many? Two or more. Enough, more than enough. One was too many.

He could be in bed, sleeping, dreaming of food. Instead, he'd gone to the castle and seen the King. And couldn't tell his father that. He might die and they never know the company he kept. No one to ever know or care. Death was coming too easily to too many.

Out here in the mud. Just another who didn't get through the lines.

The footsteps squelched off. He crawled on. Interminable night. How many more fires? Where was the river? Five minutes walk from the castle on a fine day, with bread and cheese and a fishing rod. An hour on your belly.

There were just a few more fires. And then a long patch of darkness, before faint fires began again. It must be the river between. He was close, that patch of darkness. And then the big test. Her magic. It had certainly paralysed him, exploded within him like lightning flashes – but that wasn't its promise...

'Who's there?' came a shout.

He lay still. Trembling with terror.

'Name yourself.'

Closer this time. He had been seen. There was no doubt.

No point waiting for the knife. He knew the way. Cadd rose and ran. Pell-mell, for life.

There came a chorus of shouts, to either side. He was running past the last fires. There were men with firebrands, shadows running towards him. A spear crashed to his side. Yelling, curses – another spear over his head. In the light of the firebrands he could make out the edge of the river. Fifty yards away perhaps. Feet tramping. Screaming. He dare not look back. An arrow whizzed past. Another, closer.

He ran down the bank. For a few seconds, invisible. He slipped, pulled himself up and stumbled on. Arrows were flying overhead. His lungs were bursting, but the screaming, yelling, and the barking of dogs pressed him on. He was in the water. Slowed by the thickness and cold. They were coming quickly, the sound surging towards him. Arrows and spears splashed into the water. It was to his knees, to his thighs. He dived and began a splashing swim.

He was as visible as the moon.

And then he went under water.

Chapter 7

The water was cold, but fear was warmer. Pitch black, streaming over him. He knew they must be in the water too by now, but hampered by armour and weapons. How far out would they come?

He was still underwater. She said he would be able to breathe, so all he had to do was open his mouth, and take it in. Fear engulfed him. He would take in only water if he tried to breathe. And fill up like a jug. The old witch was a fraud, her prophecy, her magic – all to fool the court and the King. Water wasn't air. Water was water.

And yet he was still swimming, frog-style, underwater. And his lungs were not bursting, as they should be. Could it be...? A few more strokes and he knew. Air was getting to him. Not through his mouth and nose, but somehow filling him. He should by now be aching for breath, the pain forcing him to surface.

But there was no pain. This was magic. The explosion in his body had given him the gift she promised.

He continued swimming for a little while, and then became fearful that he might have lost his way. He stopped, and for a few moments continued to glide. Slowly he came to a halt. Cadd could feel the river current. He was a little off true as he must cross it at right angles, but not so far off.

Without knowing, he had risen to the surface, and was suddenly aware of it. He put his head up and looked back. He was perhaps a hundred yards off the shore he had come from. In a cluster of firebrands he could see a rowing boat being pushed out. They were looking for him. Surely they would assume he was dead as he hadn't surfaced. So why bother searching for the body?

He felt for the pouch at his waist. Still there. That's what they wanted. Information on whom he was seeking, and how the siege was going. Down he went into the water. Let them do as they wished. It would be a vain search.

In a while he could hear them. Closer they came, until they were to one side of him, perhaps twelve feet off, and eight feet above. He could feel the sweep of the oars, and just make them out in the firebrand light. The boat was a long dark shadow, the oars swinging back and forth like the legs of a beetle.

They could not see him, he was sure, swimming along the bottom. Besides, they would not be looking there. Though he took the precaution of swimming along the line of the current to give himself some distance from these fishers of men.

Chapter 8

He had swum into weed, fine and wispy, like the long hair of a maiden. It curled around his limbs, neck and head as if seeking to hold him in the depths. But he was not to be held. When he stepped ashore he was like a creature from the depths, streaming with weed. He collapsed on the bank and almost blacked out. He wasn't used to swimming. Sitting down, recovering, he saw the rowing boat in its pocket of light, heading back to the other shore. With satisfaction, he realised they had given up.

As he sat, he peeled the threads off himself. And flapped his arms to generate some heat. But ceased when he saw the fires of the encampment on this side. The nearest were perhaps a hundred yards away. Along the shore, he noted a number of boats, drawn up to the bank. If he'd come prepared, he could have burnt them and then escaped into the river. But he had nothing to light a fire with.

Cadd emptied his shoes and walked cautiously along the shore, prepared, should he see anyone, to rush into the water. Although cold and weary, he was pleased with himself. He had done the difficult part of going through the lines: getting past the fires and across the river. Now he would take the long way round this encampment: go along the river and past it that way. How much time had he got before daylight? He tried to estimate. It was just after midnight when he came down the wall. He must have been crawling to the river for, say, half an hour. Crossing the river had seemed an age but it can't have taken more than fifteen minutes. So one o'clock, perhaps one thirty at the latest. This was going well. It wouldn't be light until six. He had plenty of time to be well away.

Up ahead, he spotted a fire on the riverbank. Cadd went down to the water, and swam under water until he was well past. This proved exhausting. He was swimming upriver and had to fight the current. Without knowing, he began to drift to the other side, and when at last he was past the fire, he found when he surfaced that he was in the middle of the river. He swam to the bank, taking quite a few breaks on the way. At each one he would simply stop in the water and bob up and down, just below the surface, like a waterlogged cork.

Coming ashore, he staggered up the bank as weak as a baby. If anyone spotted him now, then he'd be done for. He rested by a bush. Fortunately it was too cold to sleep, as he could easily have drifted off. Fear and tiredness battled within him. And too soon, fear pushed him on.

A little later he had, again, to swim round a fire. In the water he got cramp and it took him an age to reach the bank, with long rests between bouts of swimming. He stumbled ashore and fell after a few strides up the bank – and could hardly rise, he was so shaky and weak. Cadd rested as long as he dared. He was past the enemy lines, he was sure. Time to head inland.

He crossed a pasture, well trampled by soldiery. To his relief, at the other side was a wood. He could not go much further; it was if his limbs were hollowed out and he was boneless. He must rest. He would get into the wood, and there find a bush to hide under.

It was too dark to find a path into the wood, so he pushed his way through, attacked by shrub and bramble. Just a little further and he'd stop for the night. Not too near the edge, as soldiers might come this way for firewood.

It happened so quickly, there was nothing he could do. He trod on something metallic, heard a clang, and a jaw snapped onto his leg. The pain was at once excruciating and he screamed out. Cadd knew at once he was in a trap. It bit round the ankle and cut deep into his flesh. Blood oozed into his leggings and shoes. Perhaps he could have forced the trap open if he'd have been fresh, but in his weakened state the trap stayed shut. And Cadd bled, and that, with the pain, extracted whatever strength might have remained.

Chapter 9

He awoke in a mist, blood pumping in his ears. A grey-haired man in an ornate uniform was standing over him, going in and out of focus. The roof above was canvas. This must be a tent of sorts. There seemed to be someone else here, blurry at the edge of his sight. Cadd was on a sort of raised stretcher, pillows under his head, no blanket. His lips and throat were dry.

'Water,' he said, surprised at the croakiness of his voice.

The grey-haired man nodded, and handed him a cup. Cadd's hand was trembling so much he could not get it to his lips.

'Let me,' said the man. He took the cup and held it to Cadd's lips, who sipped greedily until the cup was empty.

Cadd felt a little better, but so weak, his eyesight fuzzy.

'Are you General Hal?' he said.

The man smiled and someone laughed.

'I am afraid not,' said the man. 'Though I am a General. General Gild. You may know of me?'

Cadd nodded. It was as he feared; he was in enemy hands.

'We have this letter,' said General Gild, holding up the yellow parchment. 'Signed by the King, I note. Matters must be desperate there.'

Cadd did not reply.

'Desperate to send someone so young,' went on the General. 'How long do you think they can hold out?'

Cadd did not reply.

The General smiled. He had a thin moustache over his top lip and a beard like an inverted pyramid hanging from his chin.

'Matters are clear enough,' he said. 'We need not torture you.'

He did not speak for a while, commencing to stroll up and down in front of Cadd stroking his beard.

'You are brave,' he said at last. 'You have done well. A pride to your King. I wish we had more of your sort amongst us.' He stopped his stroll and stood over Cadd. 'But I am afraid we must execute you.' He shrugged helplessly. 'You see – we take no prisoners.'

Cadd barely cared. The man's face was going in and out of the mist. He had failed. He couldn't think beyond the moment.

'You may wonder why you are here,' said the General. 'Why we didn't kill you on the spot. Well, the letter signed by a King gave you extra hours – though it's straightforward enough. Were you in his presence?'

'Yes, sir.' He saw no reason not to be polite to his enemy. His mother would expect it.

'It requests General Hal to come at all speed…'

The other person in the tent laughed.

'*As the town cannot hold out for more than a few weeks…*' read the General. He looked down at the young man. 'This is dire news.'

More laughter.

'What will you do to us?' said Cadd.

'What is customary,' said the General.

'I do not know your customs.'

The General smiled, the other man chuckled.

'Slaughter, rape and pillage,' said the General. 'Isn't that the custom of all armies?'

'Why?' said Cadd.

'Why?' repeated the General, wide-eyed.

'We will be defeated. Why…' he couldn't say the words.

The General helped him. 'Why slaughter, rape and pillage.'

Cadd nodded.

The General was walking with his hands behind his back. 'Not for the sake of it,' he said with a thoughtful sigh, 'but to send a message to the other towns of your country. If they surrender at once we'll be merciful. If we are forced to lay siege then we will slaughter them.'

Cadd could not fault the logic. He shivered; tears filled his eyes. His parents and his brother would be put to the sword. He had failed.

'Must you?' he said. 'Can't you be merciful?'

The General shook his head. 'I cannot. I have a duty to my own King. I have a duty to my men. How many of our lives will it cost if we have to fight our way through every town and city of your country? But with one terrible slaughter, one example. You see?'

Cadd saw. And had no wish to see.

'Please kill me,' he said.

'Shortly,' said the General. He had resumed pacing, his hands behind his back. 'You are brave. You are intelligent, but I am puzzled. You no doubt came over the wall. Lowered by a rope I expect. Well, you cannot fly. You crawled through our lines. Then you came to the river. And you were seen. Arrows and spears were aimed at you. A boat was sent after you...' he stopped. 'You must be an incredible swimmer.'

Cadd smiled.

'You evaded our weapons and a boat. How?'

Cadd smiled.

The General smiled back at him. 'I don't believe in luck in such things. How?'

'Bribery,' said Cadd.

'What?' demanded the General.

Cadd stared hard at him, having trouble holding him in focus. I'll cause them trouble before I go, he thought. Damned I will.

'I don't know who,' he said. 'I didn't do it, but certain people were bribed not to see certain things.'

The General turned away abruptly.

'What do you know of this, Loo?' he barked.

'Nothing, sir.'

'How else can a man cross the river without being seen? Begin with the boatmen...'

He was interrupted by the entry of a young man, about the same age as Cadd.

The General bowed to him. 'Your Highness.'

The visitor was ornately dressed. He had lace at the throat, a green embroidered jacket with gold buttons. He had a matching soft hat out of which poked almost-black curly hair. He was of medium height, stocky and very clean for an army camp. In his right hand was a walking stick with a silver handle and iron tip. When he walked he pressed it into the ground, as he had a slight limp.

'Where's this swimmer?' he demanded. 'This fish I hear about.'

'Here, Your Highness,' said the General, indicating Cadd on the stretcher.

'Him?' The Prince turned his nose up. 'Looks more like a worm in all that mud.' The Prince peered at him closely. 'I see no fins. Where's his tail?'

'He is a puzzle, Your Highness.'

'A filthy puzzle. Why there is always so much mud in your camps, General, amazes me. You seem to go for the biggest puddles, the heaviest clay...' As he spoke, the Prince was still looking at Cadd, as if he were an exhibit rather than a person. He snapped his fingers. 'I've seen him before. Loo?'

'Yes, Your Highness.'

'Wash his face.'

The officer grimaced; it was not one of his duties to wash prisoners. But neither was it to argue with Princes. He picked up the bucket and a cloth.

'Why should a swimmer be so mud-covered?' mused the Prince. 'Unless he crawled under the bottom...' He swung his stick and pointed the silver tip at Cadd. 'You see – a worm.'

Loo pushed up the sleeves of his jacket. He soaked the cloth in the water, wrung it out and wiped it over Cadd's face. At first he simply smeared the mud. He did it again.

'Heavens!' exclaimed the General.

'It's not possible,' said Loo, his cloth hand frozen above the bucket.

Both looked to the Prince who was staring fixedly at Cadd.

'Carry on with the clean-up,' he said. 'He may be more than a worm.'

Loo liberally applied the water to Cadd's face, ears and neck. Somewhat roughly. Cadd had to close his eyes. It reminded him of his mother. When she was in a rush, when he was smaller, and they were going to visit relatives.

The wash completed, Loo stood aside.

The General shook his head. 'I would not have believed it. The hair, the nose, the cheekbones...'

'Even the eye colour,' exclaimed the Prince. 'Look at that. The cleft on the chin...' He stopped. 'I cannot believe what I am seeing. The mudfish is a copy of me. I dare say his table manners could be improved. His hands are considerably rougher...' The Prince turned to the General. 'What do you intend doing with him?'

'He is to be executed, Your Highness.'

The Prince laughed and flipped Cadd under the chin. 'I am afraid not. I have uses for him.' He chewed a nail thoughtfully. 'Only the three of us have seen him cleaned up.'

'Yes, Your Highness.'

'No one else must know.'

The Prince was running his eyes down Cadd's body. 'He could do with a little more weight in his chest and belly. What do mudfish eat?' The Prince had got down to the legs. He lifted the right one, at which Cadd groaned.

'What's happened to his foot?'

'He lost it in a mantrap, Your Highness.'

The Prince dropped the leg and laughed deep down in his belly.

'Incredible! The detail! Even down to the leg. God could not have done better.'

Chapter 10

He lost track of the days. For at least two he had been in a fever. Must be at least ten days, he thought, since his capture; could be eleven or twelve. Even thirteen or more. No one would tell him how the siege was going. But this wasn't the worst of prisons, he admitted. The food was good, plenty of it too. The Prince wanted him fattened up – and after siege rations, mealtimes, three a day, were a highlight. Meat, real meat, potatoes, carrots shimmering in gravy. Apple puddings, jelly, custard – and a tankard of beer to wash it all down. Apparently, he was given exactly the same food as the Prince, under the Prince's orders. If he was to look like the Prince then he must eat like the Prince.

It was the copper pot over his head he hated. It was humiliating. More so even than the chain. The pot he could only remove when ordered to by the Prince, Loo or the General. It was a disguise, they said. But why the need of it? He was tied up in a tent and so few came to see him... One day he'd had enough and removed it. Loo found him in this state and threatened to whip him if he ever found him that way again. When Loo had gone, Cadd considered the situation. His aim was to escape. And so must be seen as a compliant prisoner until his opportunity came. As it must, as surely the Prince would want to use him someday soon. Or why keep him alive at all?

He'd learn to live with the pot, if he could.

At times when the pot was removed, he noted the tent was large, with a pole in the middle. He had a straw mattress and blankets too. They wanted him healthy, and to that end the healer came daily. At first twice a day. He bathed the young man's stump in some infusion of herbs and wrapped it in clean cloth. The stump end had slowly sealed over and after perhaps a week ceased to give him pain. He was given a crutch. Not that he had that much use for it. His chain was only eight feet long and he could easily hop when needs be.

The chain was attached to something outside his tent. He had tried to track it back but the chain went underground at the edge of the tent and he couldn't see far under the edge. He thought it was attached to a wagon, something like that. And had been welded onto the wide iron ring on his good ankle. All the metalwork had been a painful ordeal with the blacksmith having to work in the tent. The firing, the hammering – he'd almost died of the fumes in his pot. He felt like a performing bear, with a ring round his ankle welded to a chain. All they need do was ask him to dance. And he'd have to do that soon enough.

To the Prince's tune.

Loo came every day for an hour or so. It was his job to educate Cadd. Not reading and writing, though he could have done with that as his own was very basic, but in the necessities of the Prince's double. He learnt about the Royal family, the Prince's personal history and castles, the country of Larken: its geography, its alliances, its important people. Loo got angry when Cadd made mistakes, and would yell at him for his stupidity. Cadd suffered this without argument – but was always relieved when these sessions were over. The General came to see him a few times. His visits were civilised and more pleasant. The General liked to talk, and as he said, he was glad there was an excuse to save Cadd's life. The General told him that when the Prince felt no need of him he would probably free him. For his part, Cadd doubted this. The Prince wouldn't want a double wandering about and would probably kill him when he had no further use for him.

They were his enemy. He must not lose sight of that.

His toilet bucket was emptied regularly. And even examined by the healer, who was pleased with the latest stools. He had too much to say about the colour, the texture, the solidity. He poked them about with a stick. Not that Cadd could see, but must hear the detail of the description, as he was sightless in his pot. That damned pot. It was the bane of his life. He tried to get used to it. He told himself – what was there to see in the tent anyway? Canvas walls, the straw, the rush matting on the floor. Nothing much, but it was the imprisonment of his head – his eyes, mouth and nose – that was the greatest loss of freedom. The ring and chain might chafe but that he could accept the necessity. But not the pot. It worked on him daily, the constant humiliation – and he decided he would fight. After all they needed him.

Otherwise he'd be dead.

He began by not eating breakfast. A substantial breakfast that the Prince himself ate, consisting of bacon, eggs, kidneys, a lamb chop with fresh bread and beer. The servant took them away cold and untouched.

Neither did he eat his mid-day meal.

Loo came to see him.

'Take off your pot, Mudfish.'

He knew Loo was angry. That was when he called him Mudfish. This was to be the first battle. Slowly he took off the copper pot.

Loo was freshly shaven, his face pink and pale, his blond hair reaching to his shoulders. There was a long scar on his left cheek. Cadd had asked the General about it, knowing better than to ask Loo himself. And was told it was from a sword fighting tournament.

'What's going on?' demanded Loo.

His steely blue eyes held Cadd. His thin lips were pressed tight as he waited for a reply. Cadd knew this was it. Time to find out how much they needed him.

'I don't want to wear this pot,' he said.

Loo laughed, but there was little humour in it.

'So the prisoner is making demands.'

Cadd did not reply but held Loo's stare.

'If it was up to me, you'd be dead, Mudfish,' he hissed. 'I don't know exactly how many of your people have tried to get through our lines. A dozen or more. And if they haven't been skewered by a spear or arrow, they've had their throats cut. Post torture of course.' Loo picked up Cadd's crutch and poked him in the chest with it. 'But you are privileged, Mudfish. You eat like a prince,' he went on. 'I would give you pigs' swill and force your face into the bucket. My men eat biscuits with weevils and whatever they can scavenge. I, me, a captain,' he bashed himself on his chest, 'don't eat as well as you. A prisoner, low-born scum, a guttersnipe born of a whore. How dare you!'

During this tirade, Cadd had stared at the shackle round his ankle. Take the insults.

Without looking up, he said quietly, 'I don't want to wear this pot.'

Loo smacked him round the face. And when Cadd sat there wordless, kicked him onto his back.

'You'll wear whatever I tell you to wear!'

With a knife, Loo scraped the cold food into the copper pot.

'No one wastes food in the army, Mudfish.'

And he rammed the pot onto Cadd's head. The metal slammed on his skull, the potato and gravy rolled down his cheeks, the bone of a chop caught on his ear. And then — wham! Loo hit the pot with the crutch. Four times he smashed at the metal, making a singing stew of Cadd's brains. And would have continued – but the crutch broke.

Loo left, leaving Cadd in agony. He was sick repeatedly, though he had little to throw up. And had to take off the pot to vomit, and left it off, being past caring. He had a pulsating headache, and lay on his back clutching his head.

The healer found him that way, and commenced a clean up. The food was washed off him. His head was bandaged where it had been bleeding. And he was given an infusion for the headache – but it seemed to do little good.

The irony was, he now could not eat. Nor would the pot fit on his head with the bandage. The healer came regularly, very worried. The General came, but not Loo. Cadd gathered Loo had been admonished – which was little satisfaction as he knew Loo would find other ways to work out his hatred.

The pot quietly disappeared.

When he had recovered sufficiently, a system of signals was worked out with the General. A bell was left at the tent entrance. The General, the Prince and Loo (when he was allowed to come once more) need only call out their presence. The healer was now included on this privileged list as he had seen Cadd in his administering. Any others – servants for instance who brought the meals, changed the straw, emptied the chamber pot – and Cadd would have to turn his back until they were gone, signalled by another ringing of the bell.

The headaches went. Cadd was weaned back to food. First with soups and custard, and then more solid food. The bandage round his head was removed, and he was given a new crutch. The old regime returned, sans pot, when Loo came back. The captain was more subdued in his lessons, obviously chastised – but the resentment could be readily seen in his eyes. Neither mentioned the pot or its aftermath.

Routine commenced.

Without the pot, Cadd was freer. He made models with strings he was able to pull from the matting. And he played with them. Childish games, stories he made up, but he had lots of time to push away. He worried endlessly about his town and his family but could do even less for them than he could for himself. If he had the chance, he would yet get to General Hal – but with a chain, and a stump, that venture was on hold.

A cobbler came. Not into the tent. Cadd put his legs out the door with the flaps preventing the cobbler seeing the rest of his body. And the cobbler measured up. They had a friendly conversation, even if they could not see each other. This was the Prince's cobbler and he was to make him up two boots. One regular and one a special, like the Prince's own. He had learnt from Loo, in his lessons on the royal background, that the Prince had been born without a left foot – and so walked with the aid of the special boot and a stick. And so, it seemed, would Cadd.

The Prince would come from time to time, to joke and make fun of him, as if he were a pet monkey. Which in a way he was. The Prince would answer his questions in his disdainful way. Or not. He would examine his belly and chest to see if Cadd was gaining weight. But he did not come for three days following the incident of the pot, leaving such matters to his underlings. Though Cadd surmised he had been involved, and it was he directly who had chastised Loo. And if Loo had not been high-born, one of the ten great families – Cadd had learnt, he might be in the back of beyond scrubbing horses.

The Prince would look critically at the healing stump. Here, they were brothers. The Prince enjoyed telling him how Cadd would have to learn to walk in the new boots. How long you could walk for, and where they hurt, and what you could do to lessen it. The Prince was the expert and knew he had a willing listener, not a courtier feigning interest. One day they compared stumps. They were remarkably similar. Both on the left leg, cut off just above the ankle. The Prince showed him his boot. And incredibly, allowed him to try it on. The strapping wrapped tightly around the calf. Inside there was a wooden former for most of the foot, and a padded socket for the stump itself. Cadd's own was being made to that model.

He didn't give Cadd the other boot. Cadd would have had difficulty with it anyway because of the shackle round his ankle.

'Now walk,' commanded the Prince when the boot was on.

Cadd stood up painfully, one booted foot, one bare. He took a few steps, groaning at each one. The Prince clapped with glee like a father at a toddler's first steps.

'Now you see the need of the stick. Take it.'

Cadd took it and walked a few more paces. It was easier – but still very painful. This was going to take some getting used to. He sank to the ground in relief and untied the strapping.

'You see,' said the Prince, 'I learnt as a toddler. When I was light and small. And knew no difference. And the boots got bigger as I got bigger. Though it was fascinating to watch you.' He laughed. 'So funny to see you tottering.'

Such comments you had to take from a Prince. Besides, Cadd knew he was getting the best of treatment. And at such cosy moments, Cadd felt able to ask the Prince when he would have need of him. And the answer was always – in a few weeks. With no hint of the task.

But a few weeks came, at last. Cadd was no longer to be a monkey on a chain.

Chapter 11

The Prince came to him one morning just as Cadd was finishing his breakfast.

'Not bad grub this morning, eh?'

'Good, Your Highness.'

'The chops could be a little less fatty.'

Cadd had nothing to say on this. He thought them marvellous. And knew he would miss the food when the time came.

'Now you are to be of use,' said the Prince.

Cadd had put down his food.

'Finish up,' said the Prince.

It was difficult to eat in the Prince's presence. More difficult in his eagerness to hear the Prince's task.

'The siege still goes on,' said the Prince. 'You didn't know that,' he added at Cadd's startled response. 'It seems your people are a stubborn lot.'

Cadd said nothing, thinking – was it so stubborn to hold out against slaughter?

'Heaven knows what they are eating!' The Prince chuckled. 'Themselves I suspect. Babies first.' This amused him no end and he couldn't stop chuckling. 'Then daughters, then sons, wives… What would it be like to eat your grandparents!' He could not go on and flapped a hand helplessly in his uncontrollable mirth.

Cadd did not join in the joke, but waited for him to calm down.

The Prince wiped his eyes and mouth, as he came to himself. 'How would you cook a grandmother?' This set him off again. And it was several minutes before he was able to respond without breaking up.

'Whatever they are eating,' he smirked, but was able to hold back the laughter, 'they cannot go on much longer. The General and I are amazed they have gone this far...'

They are awaiting General Hal's relief, thought Cadd. Words he kept to himself as he swallowed the pain of them.

'Be that as it may,' went on the Prince, striding about the tent, limping slightly as he leant on the stick, 'it cannot go on much longer. And I want to be in at the kill.' He swung the stick as if it were a sword. 'That's where the glory lies. I will be the taker of the city of Tolga.'

Cadd could not evade the vision of carnage. The Prince at the head of his victorious army hacking to pieces starving people in the trapped streets, his mother and father included. Going house to house, slashing and burning. A poor sort of glory, rather cowardly – but he suspected the Prince wanted easy victory.

'So I must stay here,' went on the Prince. 'Wait it out, until Tolga falls. In the meantime my father, the King, is pressing.' He sighed deeply and waved an ineffectual hand. 'He has arranged for me to marry Princess Rosalie of Witland. Now, don't get me wrong. I agree it would make a most advantageous match. Her kingdom and ours – we could have an empire to last a millennium. But I can't be in two places at once. Hence your part.'

Cadd was in turmoil. Was he going to have to massacre his own people? Surely the Prince would not suggest that?

'You must go and seal the betrothal,' said the Prince.

Cadd felt intense relief. And then guilt. That wouldn't save his parents. Unless he could escape on the way. And even now, find General Hal...

'I have never seen her,' said the Prince. 'I do have a portrait. I know these are often idealised. Well, I've sat for a few myself. Not that I'm bad looking.' He stopped and smiled at Cadd. 'Not that *we are* bad looking. Anyway – all you have to do is go through the motions. Say yes to everything. Get betrothed on my behalf.'

Could be worse, thought Cadd. A lot worse.

'You will leave tomorrow on horseback…'

'I cannot ride a horse, Your Highness.'

The Prince waved a hand in irritation. 'You'll learn. It's a three day journey. Captain Loo will lead the guard. He'll teach you.'

It was getting worse. Loo, for heaven's sake. Away from the Prince.

'So that's that. Do a good job – and I'll do you a favour.'

'What's that, Your Highness?'

'Your people, the bakers – aren't they?'

Cadd nodded.

'I'll spare them when we take the city.'

Chapter 12

There was much to do. The boots had to be tried on for fitting, then finished off. Fortunately they fitted perfectly. Clothes had to be made ready. This was no great difficulty as the Prince had masses, even at the army camp. And the shackle had to be removed. Back came the blacksmith. This time the work was done outside the tent. Or rather the blacksmith worked outside the tent, with Cadd's leg poking through. The less who knew of the double's existence the better. Unfortunately, the blacksmith had done a sound job putting on the shackle and it took him several hours to saw through the iron ring.

Then matters proceeded swiftly. The Prince had quietly disappeared for a couple of days. And so the double could take over for this period of leave taking. Making sure he was dressed suitably, Loo took Cadd to the Prince's tents; he had in fact four, almost a courtly establishment. He had no need to walk, but was carried in the Prince's sedan chair. And once in the Prince's tent, was washed, shaved, and perfumed, with Loo sitting around as the reluctant factotum, making sure Cadd knew his part and – where not – filling in. Cadd slept in the Prince's bed. He reflected on his strange day: from shackled prisoner to prince. All the bowing and scraping, every painful step he took. Fortunately, he had to do little walking – the Prince's tent was, he was surprised to learn, almost next to his. At first all the ceremony embarrassed him, but he perfected the Prince's smile and learnt to say 'Carry on' to servants and soldiers bowing at him. Loo quietly told him to ignore the servants unless he wanted something – and as they were only underlings, manners weren't necessary. This Cadd found difficult. He was not used to servants, and saw them as people doing a job.

'Totally wrong,' said Loo. 'A servant is an inferior. So beneath a prince's vision that he is not there. Of course – expect the service, demand of them. But manners would make them uncomfortable. Be a prince. Remember, you have hundreds of servants. You can't go around greeting them, asking after their wives and children. Heavens – what world would that be! Treat them as furniture. To be moved around and sat on.'

Cadd tried it. Cushioned and laid out on one of the Prince's couches, he flicked his fingers and called out, 'Beer and cake!'

There was a scurrying and in a short while beer and cake were laid out on the low table in front of him. Much more than he could possibly eat or drink.

'Eat as little or as much as you want,' said Loo, amidst the cushions on the opposite couch. 'What happens to it afterwards is of no interest.'

Except it was. All that excess: two full cakes cut into eight slices each, pastries, a tankard of beer and a jug holding lots more, servants waiting at the door, watching to see when his plate and tankard were empty in order to refill it. His family could have lived off this for a week, and he wasn't even hungry.

For a test he flicked his finger and called out, 'Meat!'

And regretted it, for meat came. A tableful: beef, pork, chicken, venison – cutlets and chops and slices with sauces and mustards. It was like magic. The Prince demanded and it came.

One more test then.

He flicked his fingers. 'The Moon!'

There was a flurry of agitated feet and he was aware of a number of frightened faces at the entrance of his tent.

He waited.

At length a trembling servant came forward. He prostrated himself on the ground and bowed his head six times before he said a word.

'Your Almighty Highness, Protector of the Kingdom, Jewel of God – please excuse this lowly underling but my foul ears could not catch your honoured request. I would be blessed if you would command me once more.'

Cadd knew the Prince would have kicked the servant before he had finished. He, though, was somewhat sorry at the fear and consternation he had inspired. And yet he wanted to know how they might deliver the impossible.

And so, he flicked his fingers once more and said, 'The Moon.'

The servant bowed again repeatedly, and slowly rose each time bowing again, and then backed out of the tent uttering, 'Your Highness, Protector of the Kingdom, Jewel of God...'

The Moon was a long time coming. The Prince himself would have grown angry, and probably chopped a few ears off to hurry things. But Cadd waited. After all, he had cake, beer and meat to eat. And didn't know what he'd do with the Moon should it come.

Loo was not amused. Firstly as Cadd was not a real prince but a made-up baker's boy. And secondly because such use of servant time meant the other officers, that is himself and his ilk, had less use of them – as princes, of course, took precedence.

The Moon at last came. Four servants carried it in on a table. It was in fact not the Moon at all, but a huge plum cake, the size of a pregnant sow. The seas of the Moon had been drawn out with icing, and dough dragons stood here and there on its surface. At the north pole was the Prince's standard. Heaven knows how much fruit, flour and wine had gone into this monstrous pudding. It was the size of fifty such his father might make at the bakery. Used to make, he corrected himself. A long time ago. When they had flour. When they had sultanas and wine. Before they ate babies.

Lest he should break into tears in front of the servants, he flapped a princely hand.

'Take it away,' he ordered.

The servants looked to each other in concern. Was the Prince being critical? And if so, what would be the consequences?

'Take it away,' he repeated. 'Eat it!'

And the Moon was raised on its table. And disappeared rapidly, pushed away by its attendants, eager to get away from the Prince's scrutiny. Surely they couldn't eat all that, thought Cadd. But he knew they would certainly try. It was, after all, the Prince's command.

Loo had almost disappeared in his own anger. But could barely express it. He couldn't be seen to be displeased with the Prince – and to be heard yelling at the Prince would destroy the image they were protecting. He was limited to whispering his displeasure.

'Don't indulge them, baker's boy. They will become rebellious.'

At which Cadd flicked his fingers and called out in a loud voice, easily heard through tent walls:

'You are dismissed, Loo.'

And the lowly Loo bowed and skulked off.

Chapter 13

In the morning, Cadd somewhat regretted his treatment of Loo, as he needed his assistance on their journey. He was aware he could be creating a dangerous enmity. Better, he thought, if he could befriend him, or get as close as he could to that mode. He realised that Loo would find it difficult to drop the prejudice of his class – and favour a baker's boy.

At least he should try to humiliate Loo less.

In the morning he was washed and dressed, wishing there were less servants to assist – or even none at all – but a prince must be a prince. He put on the boots. He would not allow a servant to do it. A correct action – as he'd been told by the Prince that he did it himself. The servants could never get it right.

The ordinary boot was no problem. It had matching straps to the special, but they were just for show. The other he put on more slowly. Much of the inside of the shoe section was wood to simulate a foot inside. Then a lot of padding where the stump fitted, and above it a high sleeve of leather, coming halfway up the calf. This had to be made tight with straps. Before putting on the boots, he put on an especially made pair of woollen socks, one a regular sock, the other with fabric thicker under the stump to give extra cushioning. He eased his stump into the padding. He had done this often enough, with all the making and fitting – but now came the real test. The tightening of the straps was crucial, as the sleeve would take some weight off the stump which could not take the weight a foot could. Getting it right was a palaver. First time, he'd pulled the straps too tightly – causing so much pain on his calf that he had to untie them. He had to find the balance, tight enough but not too tight. And hoped there was one.

He had worn the boots the day before to get to the sedan chair, and out of it, but that was all. In all he doubted he'd walked more than fifteen paces – but even that beggarly amount was painful.

Just fifteen paces – and that was with the stick. Though he had the example of the real Prince. It could be done. In a while, he would be walking properly, he was determined, albeit with a limp. He must. He wouldn't always be a prince, followed by a sedan.

He knew too that learning to ride was crucial, especially as his walking was limited, at least for the time being. And anyway, as the Prince's double, he must ride. Princes ride, it goes without saying; it is expected. So the double must ride, but so must Cadd himself. If he was ever to escape, to get to General Hal – it wouldn't be on feet that could barely make fifteen paces.

His first riding lesson was awful. Loo had organised it an hour or two before they were due to set off. The servants were packing, the guard was making ready. Cadd was carried by sedan into a meadow where Loo waited with two horses. The servants were dismissed.

The first problem was that Cadd could not mount the horse. He tried several times but was in agony. He simply could not press down hard enough in the stirrup to raise himself. It didn't matter which foot he used – he couldn't get the force.

'I can't do it,' he said, after his fourth attempt.

'You must, baker's boy,' hissed Loo. 'The whole camp has seen the Prince ride.'

'Is there no carriage?'

'No. The Prince rides. He loves to ride. He is a great horseman.' Loo stopped, he sighed, and controlled his temper as best he could. 'Now this is the way.'

And Loo put one foot in the stirrup, gripped the saddle and easily swung his other leg over.

'Your turn.'

Cadd stood his ground. 'I can't do it.'

'You must,' yelled Loo.

Cadd sighed. He was standing on one leg using the stick as his other was hurting.

He said, 'I have one foot. I can barely walk. I'm already exhausted from my attempt at walking this morning where I extended my range to seventeen paces. I am weary. I have never ridden a horse before. Don't tell me I must.'

Loo paced about. He pulled at his chin. 'What's to be done?'

Cadd shrugged. It was obvious to him.

'I must be lifted to the saddle,' he said.

Loo turned to him, mouth agape. 'The Prince lifted? Lifted into the saddle!' He shook his head vehemently. 'It can't be done. No!' He paced in a circle, speechless with agitation, throwing his hands about. At last he said, 'You must keep trying until you can do it.'

Cadd looked up the heaven's and sighed. 'You're not listening to me, Loo. I have one foot. I am weary from the walk I attempted this morning. Perhaps I shouldn't have done it. But who's to advise me? What do you know about having one foot? Tomorrow perhaps I'll be able to mount the horse. But today I must be lifted.'

Loo had his head in his hands as he circled. 'Why must this be left to me? Why wasn't this considered?'

'Because the Prince can,' said Cadd wearily. 'And I will too. But not now.'

'But we must be on the move. We are expected.'

'Then assist me. I will stay on the horse. When I arrive back at camp, I won't dismount. We'll leave. And no one will know of my problem.'

'Yes, yes,' exclaimed Loo, seeing the way out. 'If we leave the camp with you on a horse – that will do.'

With Loo's help, Cadd was able to mount the horse. There was a holster for the stick, he noted, attached to the saddle. Some things had been thought of. But not all. Cadd was exceedingly nervous up on the horse. It was a long way down from the horse's back, and further still, or so it seemed, if you only have one foot.

With the animal motionless, the lesson went straightforwardly. Cadd's feet were placed correctly in the stirrup, he was holding the reins as instructed, and his back was upright. But the first steps, slow as they were, practically threw him off the horse – and he was clutching at the neck and mane.

In the hour that followed, Loo taught Cadd to sit in the saddle and take the bumps without falling off. Very slowly they rode together into camp. Cadd was already sore, dying to take off his boot and bathe his foot. But he had to see this through.

In camp the guard were ready. There were twelve of them with a wagon of supplies. Cadd looked enviously at the man on the seat of the wagon. And thought to himself – that's where I should be. He was utterly exhausted, the walking and riding had already taken their toll, and the journey had not even begun. If he dismounted, he would collapse.

'Move,' he hissed to Loo, 'Quickly, before I fall off this damned beast.'

The guard set off with Loo and he at the rear of the mounted guard, and the wagon just behind. The Prince and Loo's baggage train were not yet ready. Those in charge of it were instructed to hasten and to catch the Prince's party on the road. Cadd knew they would have little problem. It was as much as he could do to leave the camp, let alone put on any speed.

As they passed slowly through the avenue of huts and tents, the soldiers bowed to their Prince. Cadd raised a hand in greeting and gripped the animal with his thighs. It obediently followed those in front. All he need do was stay in the saddle. From the strain on his face, the watching soldiery may have thought he had a stomach ulcer – or at least some general displeasure with them.

It had been arranged that the next day the real Prince would return, early in the morning so no one would note his guard was different. The camp, having no idea where this party was going, would simply think the Prince had been on a short excursion. By which time Cadd would be well on the way to Witland.

Once out of the encampment, Cadd felt some relief. At least he was free of the prying eyes. That was the worst of being the Prince. Everything he did was so public. Every action had to be thought in terms of – would the Prince do this?

But in their small company, he could now take liberties.

Barely twenty minutes out, he said to Loo, 'This is killing me. I must get on the wagon.'

'You can't,' hissed Loo. 'A prince would never ride a wagon...'

'It's that or stop,' said Cadd wearily.

'Not the wagon...'

Cadd swung himself off. The horse was walking slowly – and it was certainly easier getting off than on. But once on the ground, and with one hand attached to the horse, he fell and might have even been trampled under the horse of the wagon, had the driver not been quick and pulled the horse up sharp.

Loo immediately dismounted.

'Your Highness,' he called, as the wagon driver was in earshot. 'Are you alright?'

'Get me on the wagon, Loo.' He caught his eye. 'Please.'

'Yes, Your Highness.'

It was explained to the wagon driver that the Prince was not feeling well. The driver made room, and was plainly nervous at such august company. Loo rode alongside, having tied Cadd's horse to the back of the wagon.

Cadd was relieved at getting off the horse, though he wished the board was softer as his back and haunches were stiff from riding and his earlier walking. But at least he could make himself a little more comfortable.

Loo watched in disgust as the Prince removed his boot and sock, and massaged his stump.

Chapter 14

Later in the day, Loo gave Cadd another riding lesson. The detachment were sent ahead to make camp so his humiliation would not be seen. But things went somewhat better. Although Cadd was stiff, he was less tired, having been travelling on the wagon for four hours. This time he was able to mount the horse. His good foot had to go into the stirrup and a heave up from that. Though the first time he tried, he swung himself up and ended up backwards facing the horse's rump.

Loo guffawed.

'At least I mounted it,' said Cadd, peeved at this reaction.

'If fools will ride...' laughed Loo.

Loo was not a good instructor. He was impatient, being used to giving orders and — where he wasn't obeyed — punishment. He'd been riding himself since he was a boy and had forgotten his own difficulties, or perhaps pretended he'd never had them. Loo should not have been chosen to teach a novice, but he was all Cadd had. And neither of them much liked it. The horse, though, was one of the Prince's, and had been trained from the beginning to take a rider with a weakened foot. Cadd marvelled at the mare's infinite patience.

For a good hour, Cadd mounted and dismounted until he was dizzy with the effort. Then they rode to catch up the detachment. At first a walk; Cadd could manage that. Then a trot which Cadd found difficult 'Bounce with the horse,' yelled Loo after him. After some bouncing, with and against the horse, Cadd was bounced into submission. Except it wasn't so easy slowing down the animal. It took him several tries, squeezing with his legs and gently pulling at the reins. And so the ride continued at a walk while Loo explained the elements of horse husbandry and riding – which Cadd vaguely nodded to, taking in very little. He would not have believed it was possible to be so tired. Every muscle seemed to be crying out in pain. If he could, he would have dismounted and led the horse – but walking could not be imagined either.

Loo though was eager for the lesson to go on. He wanted Cadd to practise the halt and further trotting – but Cadd refused.

'I cannot,' he said. 'I want to lay down and die.'

Loo was disgusted. 'And I'm to make a horseman of you before we get to Witland.' He threw his head back. 'You will be expected to hunt and ride with the King.'

Cadd shook his head.

Loo retorted, 'Now you'll barely keep up with the infants. What a wet-nurse of a job this is!'

Cadd sagged in the saddle, bone weary, his buttocks aching, stump itching, back and legs stiffening. He could give no argument – except the impossibility of a trot or anything requiring effort or intelligence. He was suffering on horseback.

When they reached where the detachment had fixed camp, Cadd lacked the energy to halt the horse – but a soldier, seeing his distress, took it by the reins. Cadd nodded his thanks and dismounted. And at once fell in a heap. Loo ordered assistance and two soldiers helped the Prince onto a blanket where he lay groaning. There was concern amongst them, they thought he was ill – but Loo gave no explanation. He would far rather that the Prince was sick with fever than be seen as a poor horseman.

A little later the baggage train turned up, consisting of two wagons. The four servants immediately set to and assembled the Prince's tent and bed – and gratefully he disappeared inside.

Chapter 15

The next day, Cadd did not ride. He simply could not. His body had too much to cope with: the aching stiffness from riding and his legs almost deadened with all the effort of walking. And Loo lacked any sympathy. It was his job to produce the simulacrum of a Prince – but the clay he must form resisted being moulded.

'You will disgrace us, baker's boy.'

But Cadd stayed on the wagon all day. From the gear on the baggage train, he was able to make his seat more comfortable with cushions. He had a blanket over his knee and so was able to remove his boot. He was determined not to ride that day, no matter what Loo had to say.

And he said a lot.

At last the detachment halted for the night. Cadd fastened his boots. He would practise some walking while camp was being set up. He got down from the wagon, leaving cushions and blanket behind, but taking his stick. He'd try for twenty paces.

A little later, Cadd was aware of Loo scowling as he watched him walk. Cadd bit his lip. He was in pain and temper at his efforts anyway, and the continual sniping of Loo wore him down further.

Damn the man. Pay him no heed. Try at least. Cadd rested on the stick, standing on one foot, breathing hard. He could order a chair, but knew if he sat down that would be the end of his attempt for today. To hell with Loo. He would have to deal with him, somehow. But not now. Walking had to be done. And walking was all.

And then it came to him. He was watching a horse prancing, lifting his knees. Suppose...? He'd been trying to walk the way he used to walk. But he lacked one ankle. One foot could heel-toe with each step, but the other painfully did what it could to keep going. Suppose he made things equal, rather than favour one leg. Imagine he had no ankles at all, then the other wouldn't be at a disadvantage. He must walk without any heel-toe. Put both feet down flat.

He experimented. Loo was watching, grimacing. Damn him. Cadd kept his eyes to the ground, on his feet and legs. And found that if he raised his knee, then his foot could be placed square on to the ground. When he looked up, not simply Loo was watching him, but two soldiers wiping down the horses. He glared at them, and they returned at once to full concentration on their efforts. Not that it mattered much if they looked – but it was good practise of the princely glare.

He started to walk in the new way: raising his knees and putting both feet down flat. Not onto his heels then toe which he'd been trying to do before, but a more high stepping horsy gait. And knew almost at once that he'd got it. This might be ungainly, but it worked. He wondered why he had not noted it in the Prince. And realised it was because he'd hardly seen him walk. Hadn't seen him outdoors at all, always in the confines of a tent where the Prince had barely needed to take a pace or two.

Slowly he made fifty paces. He stopped, and wanted to cheer with happiness. He had got it. He could walk again. But could not cheer. These men thought he'd always been walking, with the exception of Loo who only wanted him to ride. But his jubilation died somewhat when he saw his practice had taken him some way from his tent. Must he call for servants to carry him back? *I will get there*, he thought. So he continued. How much of his tiredness was due to walking, how much due to riding, he could not divide. But he was pushed on by knowing he could walk, would walk more – and if it was a little ungainly – well, no one criticised princes.

I will get there.

Each pace hurt his footless leg, as if hot needles were being forced up the calf through the stump. His breathing was rapid. And he was aware the whole camp was watching him. What did they think he was up to? *I will get there.*

Loo was at his side.

'What d'you think you're doing with this exhibition?' he hissed.

'I will get there,' Cadd said, eyes just ahead of his foot.

'You're not a schoolboy playing hopscotch!'

Cadd swung at Loo with his stick, striking him across his shoulder.

'Confine that man to his tent,' he yelled.

Two soldiers rushed forward, and stood bewildered by Loo and the Prince. Cadd snapped his fingers.

'Take him to his tent. Give him no meal.'

They did not need to take Loo, but followed in his wake – as Loo headed for his tent, head bowed, angry as a roped stallion.

Cadd watched him disappear into the canvas and then continued. He must do this. Nobody would stop him now. He would not ask for help. And walked on, step following aching step. He must get there.

And he sank, at last, into the chair before his tent. He pointed to his feet, unable to speak, and a servant brought a footstool. Eighty-two paces. Miraculous.

Chapter 16

As the evening came down, he lay on his bed wondering what he was going to do about Loo. He had confined him to his tent without food. That could not go on. Loo would be as furious and as dangerous as a hive of hornets.

He massaged his stump. His feet were bare, he'd washed them in warm water. Although weary, he was satisfied with his efforts that day. He could walk again, and wanted to yell it to the whole camp. But could tell no one. None of those shadows walking in the twilight. His bed faced the half-open entrance. The first stars were becoming visible above the silhouettes of the trees. But the situation with Loo oppressed him. Cadd knew he couldn't leave matters. Back on the road tomorrow, how would things go? What was he to do with the man?

He must decide tonight.

He could take Loo in irons as a prisoner. That might prove risky as Loo could start blabbing that Cadd was not the real Prince. Whether he would be believed or not would depend on whom he said it to and how Cadd behaved. A frightening prospect though. Especially if Loo was believed.

Why take the chance?

Cadd could kill him. It wouldn't be difficult, especially with Loo not expecting it. Get his own soldiers to cut his throat while he slept. The irony of that almost amused Cadd. A prince's order must be obeyed. And he was certain the Prince routinely killed those out of favour.

Of course, killing Loo would create problems later. If Cadd was not able to escape, if he had to return and explain to the Prince what had happened… Could he talk his way out of it? Maybe, maybe not. But he would be freed of Loo. And that would be a blessing. He hated him vehemently. His sneering, his criticism, the total manner of the man.

And knew it was mutual. So execution might be the only thing. Swift and sudden. Remove the problem. Then handle whatever happens later, when it happened.

Or do a deal.

Except he had no trust in Loo. Those cold blue eyes, that permanent scowl – that's why Cadd had hit him. And Loo would want vengeance. But Loo, as well as himself, was a vassal of the Prince. He needed this mission to succeed, and a dead double might mean a dead Loo. So Loo would have to swallow his pride.

Cadd convinced himself a deal could work. They need not love each other, just work together. He strapped on his boots reluctantly. He'd worn them too long today, but necessity called. And while doing so, ordered his servants to prepare food for Loo. Crossing the camp in the dusk, he refined his argument. He would make clear to Loo that it was death or agreement. No halfway compromise. Then he backtracked. If he told Loo he was considering killing him, he was warning him. Better to go for agreement, keeping silent about execution. And use it if Loo didn't keep his word.

Outside Loo's tent, the guard saluted him. Two servants arrived at this moment with trays of food. He nodded to them and told them to wait outside for his orders. He wasn't going to feed Loo until he had his agreement.

He opened the flap of the tent. It was dark inside. Probably he was sleeping. Dreaming of what he'd do to Cadd.

'Loo,' he called.

When he received no reply, he took a lantern from a servant. He shone it around the inside. The bed was undisturbed.

Loo had gone.

Chapter 17

The guard knew nothing – and was plainly terrified when questioned by Cadd. Cadd believed him; he was the least likely to have assisted Loo. The most likely to be blamed, the most likely to be hanged.

The tent had a long rip at the back where obviously, Loo had escaped. Well, easy enough to escape from a tent; it is no thick-walled prison. On reflection, he thought, if he wanted to hold him, then he should have had him bound. He was too soft in these things.

No one else knew anything about Loo's escape. Or at least, they were consistent in their stories. The second in command, the sergeant, apologised profusely. Cadd had no idea whether to believe him or anyone. A horse had gone. The guard in charge was questioned and was as terrified as a chicken in the butcher's fist. But whether he was part of the escape, or just careless, Cadd couldn't tell. All the soldiers might be in it together, saving their commander from the Prince, or Loo might have escaped by his own effort.

The real Prince would have hanged the guard at least. Cadd considered it half-heartedly, and thought if they were all in it together they might gang up on him – and kill him. They might anyway, whatever he did.

And he had no wish to hang anyone.

Loo, though, was well and truly gone. And Cadd did not miss him in the slightest. But as a precaution, he slept with four guards round his tent, considering the possibility that Loo might come back and cut his throat. Sleep came fitfully, and with bad dreams.

In the morning, he decided to ride. As far as he could anyway. He gave orders to the sergeant that they should travel slowly. And the man did not question him. It always surprised Cadd when his orders were obeyed. Just a few days ago he'd been a prisoner chained to a ring. And now he was giving orders to the same people who had imprisoned him.

He told the sergeant that he would travel at the rear, behind the wagons.

'Is that wise, Your Highness?' said the sergeant carefully.

'Are you questioning my wisdom?' said Cadd sharply.

'No, Your Highness.'

'Then to your men.'

It was in Cadd's mind, that out of sight at the back, he could more comfortably practise riding. Loo had instructed him. The rest was practice.

He let them all go from the encampment. All they left behind was the charred circle from the fire and crushed grass. The rubbish had been buried. The guard and the wagons departed, the sergeant looking back to him. And last of all, Cadd mounted his horse. At least he'd learnt that. He settled his feet in the stirrups, adjusted his position slightly. And then squeezed gently with his lower legs. To his relief, the horse began to walk behind the baggage train. Quite what he would have done if it hadn't – he did not know. He hadn't thought this totally out. And wondered too, where Loo was. Ahead of them? Gone back? Or following?

He patted the horse on her neck as she ambled on. She was a chestnut mare, chosen he was sure because she was the best-natured of the Prince's horses – and so would cope most easily with a new rider.

For an hour he kept to the walk, staying just behind the train. He noted the sergeant, riding up and down, plainly keeping an eye on him. Cadd decided he should try a trot. But first he needed distance. He must stop the horse.

He had the same difficulty he'd had two days ago. She wouldn't halt. No doubt not recognising his confused signals. This agitated Cadd which no doubt made matters worse. So he let her walk on a while. He had to be able to stop the damn animal. In two days he could be riding with the King of Witland; imagine if he couldn't halt then, with half the world watching.

He tried once more, remembering the repeated instructions of Loo: stiffen the lower back, squeeze gently with the legs and an easy pull on the reins. This time it worked. She halted. And he knew he must not rush things, nor pull too hard. But this one needed a lot of practice.

He let the train pull ahead for a few hundred yards. This would be an opportunity for Loo if he was out there, behind those trees or bushes. Most likely he was riding wildly away. Cadd fervently hoped so.

Now a trot.

He squeezed the horse's flanks with his lower legs. And miraculously, the horse began to walk. He relaxed his legs and allowed the animal to continue in this mode. Then he again squeezed with his legs and when the horse took no notice – he gently kicked with his heels. And the horse broke into a trot. And it was as if he could hear Loo's yell: rise with it.

And up and down he went as the animal lifted and fell. The track was straight, the train some way ahead – so he would not have the complication of turning the animal. Another move he'd yet have to practise. But for the time being, all he need do was stay in the saddle. And that was quite enough, as he bumped along the track.

As Cadd drew closer, he calculated when he should slow the animal. The moment came. He stiffened his back and at the same time squeezed with his legs and gently pulled in the reins. And incredibly, the animal began to walk.

He was sweating with effort and relief. The horse had responded as she should. He patted her neck gratefully. This could have gone so wrong, he thought.

He walked and trotted a couple more times until the midday halt. Did a couple of turns which didn't work out badly — but lacked the courage for a canter. On his own he might have done, but even at the rear he felt it was too public to make big mistakes.

Chapter 18

In the afternoon, Cadd, feeling more confident with his riding, rode with the soldiers. And took, like the others, the orders of the sergeant. Halting when they halted, turning when they turned. It was easy riding, without trotting or cantering – and so no opportunity for Cadd to discredit himself.

The day was cool, clouded over, and they rode through fields under a wide fishbowl sky with rolling hills along the horizon. Some of the fields were large, probably owned by the local lord and then a collection of small strips, farmed by the peasants, many of whom were in the fields with their hoes and spades. A few picking their crops, others ploughing with wooden ploughs.

Over a crest, they came into a vale and were at once hit by the most awful smell, an intensity that had them all coughing and covering their mouths and noses. The stench seemed compounded of rot, soil heaps, bad meat and standing chamber pots. Flies were everywhere.

Cadd was riding alongside the sergeant.

'I am sorry for this, Your Highness,' said the sergeant, speaking with his sleeve over his mouth. 'But there is no other way. We will be quickly through.'

Cadd's eyes were watering. 'What is it?' he said.

'The battlefield, Your Highness. Where General Hal was defeated.'

The shock almost threw Cadd from his horse.

'Defeated by whom?' he managed to say, through a cloth held to his mouth.

'By our second army, Your Highness.' The sergeant looked puzzled. 'You must remember, Your Highness. General Hal's head was taken into the camp on a pike...'

'Yes, yes of course,' said Cadd, feeling as if molten lead had been poured into his stomach. 'How far is the battlefield?'

'About a mile that way, Your Highness.' The sergeant pointed it out.

'I wish to see it,' said Cadd. 'Take me there.'

'It is not a pretty sight, Your Highness.'

Cadd nodded. He had never seen a battlefield, but did not expect anything less than horror, causing this stench and plague of flies. But he must see, must know, if the world really was changed so totally. Know if it was all over for his town.

'Order your men back over the rise,' he said, wiping the mist before his eyes. 'They need not rest in this foulness. And take me there.'

The train was sent back half a mile. And Cadd and the sergeant set off across the fields. At first at a walk, then a trot – at which Cadd had to give up the cloth over his mouth. And then into a canter. The horse obeyed each time, having the sergeant in front for his model.

They hit a fog of flies, so thick their mouths and noses filled with them. The insects crawled down their necks and into the gaps of their clothing, buzzing thickly in their ears. They at once slowed to a walk; the horses whinnied and shook their heads and bodies in discomfort. The sergeant looked back to Cadd, asking for reassurance. Cadd waved him on.

'Take me to Hell,' he said.

They came over a short rise. And saw.

They were in a field of beans. But that that was not the only crop: as far as could be seen were bodies lying amidst the crushed crop with a shroud of flies over them like fluttering muslin. Here and there, rats ran in and out of half-eaten corpses. A gathering of crows pecked at some mass, blanketing it so thickly that what it was could only be surmised. Swollen limbs, heads and hands had fresh growth spreading around them, bean pods poking into faces, dangling before hands. Armour and weapons lay scattered, already rusting. A band of dogs was tugging at a body, pulling it apart, and the entrails flopped out like jellied rope.

A flood forced up from Cadd's stomach. Unable to do otherwise, he leant over the side of his horse and vomited a white stream onto the dried crust of blood on the soil. When at last he lifted his head, his lips still dripping, the sergeant handed him a cloth.

As he wiped himself, Cadd burbled through his sour tongue, 'How long ago?'

The sergeant's eyes widened. 'Just three weeks, Your Highness.'

Cadd nodded as if he remembered. 'Yes. I lose track of time at camp.'

He was like a sunken flag, overcome with sadness. His brothers lay here somewhere, his countrymen. Their hopes were here, rotten and chewed with the corpses. His mouth was acrid and dry, his head ached. Here he was at last. He had arrived at his destination – but could not deliver the King's message. There was no one to receive it. Tears rolled down his cheek; he bit a fist to prevent himself crying out in grief.

His horse reared and almost threw him. And once he had settled it, he thought, enough. Leave this place to the rats, dogs and flies. Leave it to the rot and the rain. He turned the horse who was eager to be away, and broke into a trot at his slightest bidding. The sergeant followed. They were accompanied by a cloak of flies which would not be beaten off. Cadd's face and neck crawled with them, as if death itself had vacated the bodies on the battlefield, eager to take more life. He spat them out and squeezed them from his nose. The stink of death assailed his heart.

Once back to where they had left the trail, he told the sergeant he would ride on, while the sergeant should bring on the soldiers and the train.

They parted.

Cadd, eager to leave this valley, had his horse trot then canter. And had his riding lesson chased by flies and the reek of corpses.

Alone, he could weep freely.

Chapter 19

That night he did not leave his tent. He was in despair. There was no hope for his town. He had found General Hal's army. And they could only feed the crows. Questioning the sergeant, he learnt there were few survivors. Those that hadn't died on the battlefield, had been ridden down. A retreating army is easy meat.

Tolga would fall. It might already have; he'd been long enough getting this far. But if it still stood, it was hopeless; day after day the lookouts staring into the distance for an army that could never come.

The Prince had promised to save Cadd's family. If the Prince could be trusted, if the Prince would even remember such an insignificant detail when his army rushed in for slaughter and plunder. And even if he did, who was to say his marauding soldiers wouldn't hack off their heads, unable to distinguish one cowering family from another?

He lay stretched out on the bed, boots off. He'd been unable to eat. The universe had changed. Night was day, and day was night. He had lost heart. How could he go on? Playing the Prince, acting out a part that was never his, while his people were slaughtered. And once he had played his part – then what? To be hidden away until the Prince had another mission for him.

But who was he now anyway? Stripped of family and of country. If the very act of Prince was taken away – what remained? An empty centre, an echo of an echo, a dying smell when the plates had been removed from the table.

He must hope the siege had not fallen. Stick to that. Do just what he could. Hope that the Prince would keep his word. And to that end, Cadd must be the best of doubles. The most perfect of copies.

At dawn he rose, and went out. A heavy dew lay on the grass, the orange sun was resting on the horizon. Two soldiers were lighting a smoky fire as he walked in the morning chill. Birds were singing as if they had not heard yet of General Hal's defeat. He walked on, out of the camp, not counting paces, but went far enough to know he was a walking Prince.

And he could ride a little.

He must achieve this mission. It had changed from his original task; General Hal was dead. He could give him no message. But his parents could be saved. The Prince had promised him that if his mission was successful. And so he must succeed. He must be accepted in Witland as the Prince. And he must woo the Princess.

He must go on. There was no other way. If he escaped then his parents would be killed. And so there could be no escape — other than by doing it badly. And suffering the consequences. One side or the other would kill him then. The Prince for failing him, and Witland for his deception. So he must not fail.

He must be the Prince.

Chapter 20

He was unable to speak to anyone in the morning. But the Prince was known to be moody. And when he was, all should avoid him. So the men gave him a wide berth, while the servants made their enquiries as to his food and comforts and scuttled away, glad to be out of his range. Cadd ate a little and when they set off he rode behind the wagons. Without trying, he rode well, his weariness preventing him from straining against the horse.

Loo would be proud of him. Wherever Loo was. He had barely thought of him since seeing the battlefield. But there was a bad enemy he had made. What was he even now plotting? Cadd had an uncomfortable thought. Maybe the Prince had sent him with Cadd on purpose. Not trusting the man. Getting a potential backstabber out of the way. Cadd shrugged. What difference did it make? Loo was wherever he was. He himself must fulfil this mission. And do it so well, that if Loo were listened to – he would not be heeded.

So far it had been easy. He had only these soldiers to fool. And even if they had doubts, which wasn't likely, they didn't matter. They were underlings. The King, the Princess of Witland and the courtiers would be a different matter.

And soon he was to meet them.

The sergeant had sent two men ahead to inform the King of the Prince's arrival. Late in the morning, they returned. With them was an open carriage with a dwarf as driver, and an equerry on horseback to lead them in.

Cadd stopped the train. While the midday meal was prepared, a screen was set up for him. And he washed and changed behind it. This had all been discussed with Loo and the Prince in the days at camp. The meetings and greetings. All the ceremony that made a prince a prince and not a baker's boy.

His servant selected a green and red doublet with lace around the collar. His hose too was green and tied with string at the waist beneath the tails of the doublet. His hat matched, soft velvet, half green half red. He was the essence of a joyful prince, the last thing he felt. And was all for stripping it off and beginning again. But he must wear something. And the Prince had versed the servants on the correct apparel for this first meeting. And so he was dressed as the Prince would dress; a green and red dandy to greet the King and woo the Princess.

He ate a little. Some bread, cheese, a sip of beer but could summon no appetite. He still carried the vision of the battlefield. And, even without it, was terrified of meeting the King of Witland. Surely, he would see at once Cadd was no prince and have him cut down on the spot?

He was so ill-prepared. The Prince and Loo had not dealt with a double before and had not thought out clearly his needs. They had skimmed over the surface of being a prince, and left Cadd with the terror that lack of detail would catch him out, and reveal him as an impostor. But ill-prepared or otherwise – there could be no turning back.

The equerry bowed him into the carriage. Cadd did not know what to say to him. What was his rank? And so he decided to say nothing, which seemed to content the equerry who swept and bowed and almost Your Highnessed him to death, bending so low his head must have banged into his knees. And, even when Cadd was sitting down and comfortable, presenting him with cushions and more cushions, although the carriage was well padded. At last, to Cadd's relief, he stopped, backed away bowing, and mounted his horse. With a final bow on horseback, he took his place in front of the carriage and led off. The dwarf driver cracked his whip over the black horse and followed slowly after. With relief, Cadd stretched out...

And waited.

Chapter 21

It was not a comfortable ride in the carriage. The vehicle had been built for show, for state occasions in town streets. Here it bumped along the pot holes, where a ride on horseback would have been easier as the animal would have avoided the obstacles. But a prince must arrive like a prince. With more confidence, Cadd might have taken to horseback until the last minute – but he was in no mood to disturb matters. And so he was tossed from side to side as the trail wound its way to the King's castle.

After an hour or so, the equerry begged leave to ride ahead and prepare the castle.

'Go,' said Cadd.

And the equerry bowed deeply several times – while Cadd thought in terror, will I have to do all this before the King? Finally, the equerry turned his horse and rode off. Cadd watched him ride away, galloping fast in a cloud of dust, so he would have time to complete his bowing before the King, in time for Cadd's arrival.

'Does everyone bow so much in your country?' he said to the dwarf's back.

'It is not my country, Your Highness,' said the dwarf. 'But yes, everyone bows – and if you are not sure, then bow some more. You'll soon get used to it, Your Highness.'

'What country are you from?' said Cadd.

'I am from Viland, which is now a subject state of Witland. I would have been slaughtered but I was able to amuse the General with my tumbling and juggling – so I was saved and presented as a gift to the King.'

'You are a slave?' said Cadd, somewhat surprised at the handing over of dwarfs as presents.

'I am, Your Highness. Well treated mostly, but slavery is still slavery. And I have felt the Royal boot too many times when I failed to amuse.'

It was this admission that caused it. As Cadd too was a slave, but not one who could admit his slavery. He enjoyed the straightforward talking of the dwarf, his honesty, though he feared it could get the little man in trouble. Instinctively he felt he could trust him, unlike the equerry who was all show. So he climbed over the seat and sat by the dwarf, who didn't seem too surprised.

'My name is Bild, Your Highness.'

'Pleased to meet you, Bild.'

Bild was about three and half feet tall. He was dressed smartly in red and yellow, the clothes obviously tailored for him. His head was rather large, his nose looked as if it had been broken which was perhaps accounted for by his tumbling activities. It was difficult to tell his age, he had no grey hair – he certainly wasn't old but he wasn't young either. His hands were powerful and held the reins easily.

'I mean no rudeness, Bild,' said Cadd, 'but why should the King send his slave out to greet a prince?'

'Perhaps he thought I would amuse you.'

Cadd shook his head at this. 'I think the King ill uses you.'

'It is kind of you to say so, Your Highness.'

'What will he do when he tires of you?'

Bild shrugged. 'Depends how tired he becomes. He might free me or he might chop my head off for a final amusement.'

'The King is a savage!'

Bild put a finger to his lips. 'You may say that to me, Your Highness, but do not say that in Witland.'

'I go from one savagery to another,' sighed Cadd.

Bild turned to him, 'Excuse me saying so, Your Highness – but you don't seem very princely to me.'

'Why?'

'Well, sitting up here with me for one thing. Treating me as an equal… I'm just the King's slave. I juggle, I tumble, I deliver messages…'

'But you know things.'

'I do, but you are the only one of the three that knows so.'

'Three? Three what?'

'Princess Rosalie has three suitors. You've all been invited at the same time.'

'I didn't realise this was a competition.'

'It most certainly is. Princess Rosalie won't take just anyone. And nor will her father.'

'What's she like?'

'I like her. She has always been very kind to me.' He beamed at the thought. 'Oh – she's a wonderful young lady. The only one in the Royal household worth a bean. Don't listen to anything other people say about her. See her with an open mind. And I'll say no more.'

'Why do you speak so freely with me?'

'Because,' said Bild, 'I sense I can trust you.'

'I thought that about you.'

'Be careful, Your Highness. Don't be too trusting. There are many who pretend at court in order to lead you to say things they can use against you.'

Cadd considered this. He could be too easily caught out. And who on earth would defend him?

'I shall take heed,' he said. 'I am sure the advice is sound. But tell me – I didn't realise there were three of us. How are we to compete?'

'There will be tasks. Competitions.'

'I fear I'll be awful at them,' said Cadd, thinking of the Princely things he couldn't do. Like riding, or for heaven's sake – sword fighting. Or even writing – suppose he was asked to write a love poem to the Princess? His writing was awful, his spelling atrocious. Or play the lute. It wasn't likely he'd be asked to bake a loaf.

'Is there anything you are very good at?' said Bild.

Cadd thought, no, he couldn't say baking, even to Bild. Instead he said, 'I can swim underwater better than anyone.'

Bild smiled, his upper teeth pressed over his lower. Tumbling, wondered Cadd.

'I shall see what I can do,' mused Bild.

They came out of a clump of forest and there, a few miles ahead on a hill, was the castle. It had high walls, six white towers gleaming in the sunshine with several flags flying from the tallest tower: the flag of Witland and, he surmised, that of Larken, the Prince's own land. And maybe the flags of the other two suitors, whoever they were. The goal of his mission was to begin the linking of the two monarchies, which might ultimately result in the uniting of Witland and Larken themselves. Or might not at all, as there were other suitors for the Princess' hand.

And it might save his parents. Or not.

Thinking this way overwhelmed Cadd. It was incredible that the Prince had dared send him in his stead. Surely his father, the King of Larken, didn't know? A substitute being sent to the castle of a powerful neighbouring King, and even more heinously, to seek the hand of the Princess in a competition. Wars were fought for less. If the Prince's father ever found out, he would be enraged. A matter of state so important, treated so lightly; Cadd's life would not be worth a candle flame.

He was to be placed in competition with real princes. They born to it, he with a few ill-thought-out lessons. It was nonsense. How could he get away with it, he thought, as the carriage bumped slowly towards the castle, like a bullock walking willingly to the slaughterhouse.

'I suggest, Your Highness,' said Bild, 'that you take your place at the rear of the carriage.'

Cadd nodded and climbed back over, saying as he did so, 'Thank you for your comments.'

'It has been a pleasure, Your Highness. But now I think it best if we no longer speak as it may be misconstrued by those we approach.'

'I understand, Bild. But I do hope we can speak again.'

'And I, Your Highness.'

With that, conversation between them ceased. A prince must be a prince and a slave must be a slave. And, as if a refrain to that thought, Cadd could hear trumpeting on the wind. He could make out people leaving the castle gates. Crowds of them. All come for him? Surely not?

But as the carriage closed in, it become obvious that he was their attraction. Ahead of him people lined the widening road and stood along the castle walls. All of the castle it seemed, and the villages attending it, had come to greet Prince Grude of Larken, the honoured guest of their King. Cadd watched in horror as his carriage unhurriedly traversed the distance between himself and the bannered crowd. The journey was now less jarring as the road was good, allowing the coach to roll smoothly in, led by the high-stepping black horse.

He wanted to run from the coach, not continue into the lair of the beast. Or for the coach to go infinitely slowly, so the space between himself and the castle would stay the same. But slowly the carriage progressed. The blur of the crowd became waving people. They had colour and faces.

The trumpets sounded a long welcome. Cadd was sweating, his stump itching. And his teeth chattered in fear as the crowd cheered him in.

The coach kept to its stately pace. The people must wait, royalty would not be rushed. He tried breathing regularly, he wiped his sweaty palms. He wanted to take off his boot. Instead he sat upright and held up his hand in a regal wave as he reached the edge of the crowd. And the cheering built up to a crescendo.

The people were held in check by soldiers on foot and on horseback. Cadd kept his slow wave going, gazing alternatively from side to side at the jubilant faces. He wondered what they really thought of him, perhaps the cheering was genuine, or perhaps it was better to cheer than be whipped. He tried smiling, but his face was stiff, and refused to make one, beyond a flabby stretching of his mouth. So he gave up, and simply waved, his hand growing increasingly stiff. He switched hands.

The coach stopped. He'd not been looking ahead, but along the crowds on either side. But now he did so. By the castle gates were two lines of men in red and blue uniforms with long straight trumpets to their lips, which they now blew in a great fanfare.

And alone, out of the wide gates, to the swelling fanfare, came a portly man on a white horse, riding slowly and deliberately towards them.

It could only be the King.

The cheering was deafening. About ten yards from the coach, the horse halted and the King dismounted. Two equerries rushed in to hold the horse. The King stood still and waited.

The fanfare stopped. Those nearby in the crowd quietened. And the silence was picked up along the road, the sound dying in a wave, to the last ripples at the very end of the crowd.

Cadd had had training at least for this and knew what to do. He went to open the door of the carriage but an equerry completed the action with a low bow. Cadd stepped out. He approached the King, stopped a few paces before him and bowed low.

'I bring the greetings of Larken, Your Majesty, to your great country.'

He bowed three times.

'I humbly represent my father, the King,' he went on, 'and am honoured to be in the presence of a King so mighty and so adored.'

This had all sounded rather much when Loo had first instructed him in the greeting. But there was more of it. And he hoped it was having the desired effect.

'Your armies are glorious, Your Majesty, your victories renowned, your...' and then he dried. Your what? He had forgotten. How did it go? It wouldn't come, so he plucked words from the air. 'Your horses, your castles, your farms, your towns, your beaches, your mountains are...' Are what? Mumble, mumble. His neck was prickling, he was shaky on his feet, every eye on him, every ear straining – and the eyes of the King piercing him, his mouth drooping into displeasure. '...Are famous.' Oh how feeble! 'Are sung by the minstrels and blessed by God and his angels. I am most honoured, your exalted Majesty, to be in your presence. My father sends greetings...'

Cadd was suddenly aware he was repeating himself, and stopped. Would that do? He couldn't see the King, he was bowing so low. That 'God and his angels' phrase hadn't been taught to him by Loo or the Prince. Might the King not find it insulting? At last, feeling he had been humble long enough, he came up from his bow to face the King.

The King was standing steadfast, his hands on his hips, his legs quite wide apart, as if he were about to issue a challenge. He was fat, but he knew he had power, the power of this castle and all these people and soldiers. The power to elevate, the power to trample, the power to snuff out a life. Those stubby ringed fingers in a flick could knight or hang. He wore a black cloak open at the front, revealing a red waistcoat embroidered with gold thread, and on his head was a cloth cap to match. His hose was white and his shoes black leather with silver buckles. His face was round, unmoving, the nose thick and bulbous, and he glared from deepset eyes without blinking at Cadd.

Cadd shrivelled in the glare. What was that silly stuff about mountains and beaches? He bowed once more.

'I am honoured to be in your regal presence, Your Majesty.'

At which the King smiled. He stepped forward and embraced Cadd in powerful arms.

'Welcome to Witland, Prince Grude.'

And almost pressed the breath out of him.

Chapter 22

The King joined Cadd in his carriage, and to tumultuous cheers they were driven the final few hundred yards into the castle. Once in the courtyard the King informed Cadd there would be a banquet in the evening, and made his farewells. Cadd began his own but the King was already striding away, chased by his minions, leaving Cadd with a mouthful of victories and famous castles beloved by God.

It was, though, a relief to be abandoned. He suspected the King was bored by him; he must get an awful lot of this. And in the end when everyone sings your praises to the skies – what meaning does it have?

But boredom was at least safe. You might be avoided, but you don't get beheaded for it. He wondered how the Prince himself might have performed. As fluffy and flummoxed? Maybe. He was more practised – but Cadd was sure he could be as obsequious as a beetle at the foot of a giant, should there be anything in it for him.

A liveried servant took him to the chambers reserved for him. On the way, he asked about the soldiers of the detachment and was told that the King did not allow foreign soldiers within the castle. They must camp outside. Cadd was unsure whether this was good or bad. Certainly, he did not miss their presence – but they were intended for his protection. But then as a prince and royal suitor, why should he need it? And as an impostor – no one would help him.

The chamber was a large, well laid out room, with two smaller rooms off it, one a bedroom, the other for whatever he wished it to be. In the main room, the long draperies were open and sunlight streamed in; there were flowers on the chests in tall jugs around the room. In the centre was a rich carpet, and around it several couches fully cushioned.

More space than Cadd had ever had. Whether this was the usual sumptuousness for the Prince, he could not say – but it certainly was overwhelming for him.

A basin of warm water with rose petals floating on top was on one of the chests. By its side was a full jug, still steaming, along with a towel and soap. Cadd dismissed the King's servant and his own, saying he did not wish to be disturbed until he need prepare for the banquet, several hours away.

And he was left in peace.

He tore off the boots and socks. Sitting on a stool, he bathed his foot and stump in the warm water. His stump was red and painful. He massaged it and sighed with relief at being alone to do it. The end had completely healed. For a while it had seeped blood when he put any pressure on it, but now skin had covered the lumpy extremity.

The warm water was wonderful. The scent of rose petals filled him with hope. Gently he soaped his feet and stump. And let them luxuriate in the heat. At last he had arrived. And, on the journey, had learnt to walk far enough, which need never be that far for a prince. He was, he thought, a passable rider, but no doubt that would be tested. He hoped not too severely.

But that was another day.

After he'd washed his feet, he wanted to wash his face and hands, but not in the same dirty water. What was he to do with the waste? He could of course call a servant and get one of them to take it away – but he didn't want anyone to disturb him. He hopped about looking for a bucket. There was none.

Could he throw the water out the window?

The window was wide and open. There were only a few in the courtyard below. If he was quick... He had some difficulty hopping with the basin, and so assisted himself by taking it from surface to surface. Cadd took a quick glance out of the window, and tipped the scummy water out.

From directly below there came a scream of displeasure.

Perhaps Cadd should have drawn in quickly, but instead he looked down. And saw looking up at him, his hat and doublet drenched – Loo.

Quite who was the more surprised...

'You!' shrieked Loo.

His presence rendered Cadd speechless. But he knew he must say something. Others were looking up at him. He was recognised.

'I am a prince,' he said sternly. 'Kindly address me as such or you shall be arrested.'

Loo's fists were clenched, but he too was aware of the observers. He grimaced and wiped his plastered hair. And then bowed.

'Your Highness. It is my fault entirely.'

'In future don't listen at windows,' said Cadd and withdrew into the room.

He slammed the window shut. Out of necessity, so his laughter would not be heard. Loo's face, that just-washed surprise. Oh dear. He would never be forgiven now.

But it kept him chuckling for half an hour.

Chapter 23

Cadd tried to sleep for an hour, but rolled about restlessly. The image of the soaking Loo didn't help. Nor thoughts of what the captain was doing here, what he might have been saying. The very fact that Loo felt it safe enough to be here, troubled him.

But the King had greeted Cadd, accepted him before his people. No doubt Loo had watched his reception in the crowd. Surely that would subdue any plans he had?

He must hope so.

A servant came to wake him to prepare for the banquet, but he was already awake. New clothes were laid out for him. Cadd said he would dress himself. The servant looked surprised but Cadd had learnt their surprise didn't count. It was that of their masters he must watch out for.

But all this dressing and undressing. At home he wore the same clothes for a week or more. The thought squashed him. How were matters there? Had Tolga fallen? Were his parents and Jel alive? Here he was dressing for a banquet – and perhaps at this very instant his family and townspeople were being put to the sword.

It seemed so far away. It seemed so close.

He had an idea as he dressed. He would send one of the sergeant's men back to camp to get news. It might have taken him three days to get here, but the journey had been slow. A man hurrying, surely he could do it in a day and a half. Then return – say in three days. He'd send him tomorrow.

But why wait?

Get the messenger on the move. As it was, he'd not hear for three days. Stupid to let a whole night pass and delay matters.

His thoughts were interrupted by a rapping on the door. His dressing was almost complete; he felt respectable enough to receive visitors.

'Come in,' he called.

It was a soldier, sweaty and dirty from the trail. He bowed deeply.

'Your Highness, I have a message for you.'

He took from a pouch a grimy parchment. Cadd took it. It was sealed with the General's seal. He opened it, and had some trouble reading it. Partly due to the handwriting and partly because he was unpractised.

It was written by the Prince, but of course could not have his seal, because why give the Prince's document to the Prince? He wondered how much the messenger knew. If the Prince had given him the message, or even if the messenger had just seen him around camp – he must at least wonder what another one was doing in Witland. Or was he among the trusted few? Cadd looked up and caught fear in the man's eye. Oh, thought Cadd, I don't have much hope for your survival. It doesn't pay to know of two Princes. He returned to the letter. The Prince's scrawl wasn't much better than his own, and he was sure some of the words were spelt wrong. Or maybe not.

There was a pre-amble about Cadd's health and how well his mission was being achieved and then the important lines:

Tolga has fallen. Your family are safe and will be kept safe if you succeed. I am looking after them personally. Their continued safety depends on you.

He sank onto a couch, his heart beating rapidly. And could not speak. He had been thinking of these very things moments before. Even sending a messenger to receive the message he was now reading. Was this magic or coincidence? Safe. He bowed his head and closed his eyes –

and wondered about the Prince looking after his family personally. Did that mean a dungeon – or what?

But it could all be lies. The Prince was a practised liar. Did it all the time. Enjoyed it.

He looked up; the messenger was still standing there, awaiting his orders.

Cadd cleared his throat. 'Water please.'

He pointed it out. And the messenger hurried over to the low table and poured him a cup. He brought it back, his hand shaking.

Cadd drank deeply. 'Thank you. Now…' He took a deep breath to control his feelings. 'Tell me – what's the situation at Tolga?'

'It's fallen, Your Majesty. The day before I left.'

He watched the messenger closely as he spoke. He didn't seem to be lying, and would the Prince have thought to brief such an inferior? Not likely, he was pretty careless in most matters. Take his own training, for instance.

'And what of the people?' asked Cadd, and added in just in case he wasn't clear, 'Of Tolga.'

He waited in trepidation for the worst.

'Slaughtered, Your Highness.'

'All of them?' he exclaimed.

'Well,' said the messenger, 'I heard of a family. A baker's. No one to touch them on pain of death. But everyone else.'

'Do you know why the baker was saved?'

The messenger shrugged. 'Orders, Your Highness. That's all I know. A detachment went off to get the family, while the rest set to…'

Cadd held up a hand to stop him. 'Enough.' He could imagine the terror too well. 'Do you know where they are? This family.'

The man shook his head. 'No, Your Highness.'

A good touch that. And convincing to Cadd. The messenger only knew a little. And surely the Prince would have briefed him in a full lie – if he meant to. So it had happened. His family in a dungeon or wherever at the Prince's pleasure. While he must enjoy the King's banquet.

'Thank you,' he said at last. 'You may go.'

'Your Highness.' The man bowed and turned to leave.

'One thing,' added Cadd.

'Your Highness?'

Cadd licked his lips. He was unsure, but couldn't leave the man this way.

'Don't go back,' he said.

Fear cracked the messenger's face.

'Do you know why I am saying this?'

The man nodded. He was trembling. 'I think so, Your Majesty.'

'You will be killed for what you know,' said Cadd.

The man looked wildly about him.

'What should I do?'

'Go to the Prince's detachment camped by the city walls. Stay with them the night. Then take food for the journey back tomorrow. Say you have an urgent message from me. Then leave.' Cadd paused and shook his head. 'And go anywhere – but back.'

The man nodded.

'You're not the Prince, are you, sir?'

'No.'

'Whoever you are – thank you.'

Cadd held out his hand. And the man took it.

'I wish you luck,' said Cadd. 'And hope you will not die for knowing me. Now go.'

The man withdrew his hand, unsure whether to bow or not. And did so. He backed out of the room, plainly confused.

Cadd hoped the messenger could keep control. Or he would make the sergeant suspicious. But he'd done all he could for him. And wondered why. Had the man been amongst those who slaughtered his town? He hadn't asked. Didn't want to know. His family were at least still alive. Heaven knows where they were. But alive. And dependent on him.

He had better do a good job.

Chapter 24

Musicians were playing, but could barely be heard above the cacophony of speech and eating. Cadd was seated on a low dais. Their table, the top table, seated only five, all on one side, facing the hall: two princes, himself the outside of the two, the King, the Queen and the third prince. The princes were his fellow suitors. In the belly of the hall were parallel lines of long tables, full of the nobility, running away from them to the far end of the hall. On one of them he had noted Loo.

He had also seen Bild, who was juggling and tumbling in the floor of the hall. He could handle three balls easily, then four without trouble. His tumbling was good too. And his fire-eating was spectacular, knowing exactly how far he could spit the flame – the guests enjoying being terrorised. And for a break he clowned, mock-juggled and fell about. Cadd was surprised at how much was expected of the dwarf. He continued through the dinner. Sometimes Cadd would lose sight of him among the tables and their eaters, but then see him once more in a spurt of fire. He wondered whether Bild would get any dinner. But later on the King gave him a platter with some food on it, the treatment reminiscent of a favoured dog. Bild sat down at the edge of the dais and ate his master's leavings.

The meal consisted totally of meat. All washed down with copious goblets of wine. Servants came round with huge platters of chops, of chicken legs and assorted viands. The King was served first and he plunged in, taking what he wanted with his bare hands. Others were more delicate and used a knife or fork or both. Cadd decided to take his manners from the King. He grabbed a hot, sticky chicken leg, and placed it on the pile of veal and venison on his plate. He forked on to this slices of beef, some fried liver and a pork chop as they came round in turn. Quite how he was to eat it all he had no idea, as he had little appetite after his recent news – but knew an empty plate was rudeness.

He wondered whether being the end prince was a slight or just the way it worked out. Not that he minded not sitting next to the King or Queen. Talking to either of them would be an uncomfortable affair. There was no one to his left, and to his right was Prince Adol of Hoik, if he heard his name and country correctly amidst the racket.

Prince Adol was keen to engage him in conversation. He asked Cadd something which he could not hear. And had to ask him to repeat it. And then, embarrassingly, again.

Adol yelled into his ear. 'How many castles has your father?'

Cadd didn't know. He had been told by Loo, but had forgotten in the pile of information heaped on him. He could perhaps pretend he hadn't heard – but he realised Adol would persist.

'Five,' he yelled into Adol's ear.

Adol finished his mouthful of chicken.

'I thought it was seven,' he shouted.

Cadd now had his mouth full of liver, and thought about this. Adol was asking him questions he already knew the answer to. Strange.

'It might be seven,' he bawled, as if he was always so careless as to the number of his father's castles.

Adol then told him the names of the seven. Cadd was amazed that Adol was so well primed, especially as he knew nothing about Adol. Had never even heard of Hoik, if that was its proper name. Should he have done?

He found the best way to evade Adol's questions was to keep eating, then what with the noise and Cadd's full mouth Adol in his turn couldn't understand the answers. And keep the wine flowing, which was the only way to manage all that flesh. But it was an effort getting down all that meat. The honeyed chicken wings made his hands sticky. Cadd would have liked to have wiped his hands, but took his cue from the King who licked his fingers and wiped them on his waistcoat.

Cadd was curious about the third prince but could hardly see him, hidden as he was by the King and Queen. He could hardly in fact see the Queen, as the portly body of the King virtually occluded her. But where was the Princess?

He could of course ask Adol, but that might result in Adol wondering why he didn't know, and then asking more questions of Cadd which Adol already knew the answers to. It was enough to know she wasn't here, unless in the body of the hall – and surely that was most unlikely. She was the heir to the throne, the reason why he was here in the first place. But had his Prince really not known about the other suitors? Surely he would have come himself if he had? Unless he feared humiliation.

The King was wading through a massive pile of steak, sausages, chops and various slices of various meats and lumps of offal, tearing the pieces of meat in his fat ringed fingers. His face and beard were greasy and he talked with his mouth full. He threw a half chewed bone to Bild. Then half turned and flicked his fingers. A servant ran in with a bucket. The King vomited into it, the rest of the table totally ignoring the splurge. When the King's head lifted, the bucket was rushed away and another servant ran with a towel and wiped the royal mouth, rather like the royal barber wiping off the last of the shaving soap. The King swilled out his mouth with wine and spat it into a spittoon at his feet. And then, refreshed, returned to his meal.

It wasn't so long before Cadd was obliged to do the same. The mass of meat was gurgling in his stomach, he could not contain it. In panic he flicked his fingers, and was just able to hold it as the bucket ran in. And, head down, let it flood. Out poured lumps of chicken, pork chops, liver, beef and various unidentifiable bits, pickled in red wine and the fluids of his stomach. Unburdened, dribbling at the chin, he surfaced, the bucket went away and his mouth was wiped. He gargled away the sourness in wine and spat it into the spittoon at his feet. Cleared out, with a clean mouth, he took a deep breath and saw the King smiling approvingly at him. He was obviously looking for a hearty appetite in a future son-in-law. Not to be left out, Prince Adol joined in the ritual and the other prince too, and flicked their fingers for the buckets. And gurgled out their dinner. It was as if the tests had already begun, but unannounced. Nor the strict terms of victory proclaimed, but which certainly involved eating, drinking, vomiting, eating, drinking, vomiting… Though it was apparent to Cadd that after a couple of vomits no one was keeping score – or if there was a scorer he would be too drunk to be reliable.

Cadd was suddenly aware that he was enjoying himself. Disturbing things had happened elsewhere in the world but he couldn't remember what they were – and so they couldn't be important. He had his arm round Adol's shoulder and they were all playing a game. A partridge was passed along their line, and each had to carve off a lump with a knife and feed it to his neighbour on a knife point which was great fun as they were all very drunk, their hands slippery with grease and the knives threatening. And when the Queen dropped the partridge carcass and it slipped into the spittoon, they all laughed uproarously, and the more so as she had to get it out, spit- and wine-soaked, and carve off the piece to feed to her neighbour, the far-end prince whose face cringed in distaste.

It was during the game of flip the sausage, which involved a large chop as bat and a sausage as ball, that Cadd's head fell down on to his platter. The others were very amused and decorated the fallen head with liver, chicken wings, and a ring of gravy-soaked meat balls. They altered the game, the object now being to flip the sausage onto Cadd's prone head. But Cadd, face down in his plate of chicken wings and meat balls, smiling benignly as the sausages bounced off his head, heard no more, saw no more — as the jollity continued all about him.

Chapter 25

Cadd groaned and lifted his head. Where was he? He was flat out in a shadowy room, his head pounding, his mouth dry and leathery. He ached all over. His stomach was doing strange things, even now reluctant to hang on to its burden of meat. For a few seconds he thought he was alone – but then in the gloom he saw Bild. The dwarf was sitting on a stool, by a chest on which stood a flickering oil lamp, the only light in the room.

He knew then he was on his bed. Still fully clothed, except his boots had been taken off.

'Did I disgrace myself?' he said feebly.

'No worse than anyone else,' said Bild.

'How did I get back?'

'I brought you back with a servant.' The light and shadow were playing on the dwarf's face, one half was in light, the eye twinkling, the other barely visible. 'I cleaned you up,' added Bild. 'You were rather meaty.'

'I want to die,' grunted Cadd, pressing his forehead with both palms.

'I'm not here as a night nurse,' said Bild. 'I must leave you in a few minutes. But I came to warn you.'

'About what?' Cadd half sat up, groaned and fell back down.

'You have enemies here.'

'I know. Captain Loo.'

His head was pounding. He gripped his temples in his palms and pushed.

The dwarf pulled Cadd's hands away from his face. 'Listen to me. Deal with your hangover later. I should not be here.'

Cadd, chastened, sat up. 'Sorry,' he mumbled.

Bild sat on the bed. 'I go places, I listen. They think I'm stupid, because I'm small and I juggle. They treat me like a pet dog.'

Cadd nodded. He had seen it in the hall.

'Captain Loo is saying things against you.'

'What is he saying?'

The dwarf spoke slowly and deliberately. 'That you are not a prince at all.'

Cadd looked up in alarm. 'And is he believed?'

Bild shrugged. 'Let's say he has powerful friends. His cousin is the King's mistress. You saw her this evening with the King.'

'I thought that was the Queen.'

'The Queen doesn't come to court anymore,' said Bild. 'She is shamed by the King. But that doesn't matter to you. What does matter is that Loo has been speaking to the King's mistress, Lady Lula. I heard them while I was balancing a stick on my nose and juggling apples. She said she will talk to the King...'

'Will he believe her?'

Bild shrugged. 'Maybe. Maybe not. But he will be suspicious and will watch you. He will send to Larken for affirmation.'

'I will be affirmed,' said Cadd, unsure even as he said it. Can a prince affirm himself? Might they just dump him? If so – then Cadd's life would not be worth a fig.

'I must go,' said the dwarf. He jumped off the bed onto the floor. 'I don't know what you are. I don't care.' He made his way to the door of the room. 'All I can say is that you may have to leave in a hurry.'

And with that he was gone.

Chapter 26

Cadd could not sleep. With a hangover, and clamouring with thoughts, it was not possible. He wondered whether he should try to escape. But even getting out the castle would be difficult enough. And how far would he get on the road without a horse? Because they would come for him. Leaving would be proof of guilt.

And what would happen to his parents?

But if he couldn't save them – shouldn't he save himself? Bild's warning wasn't so helpful. It was like being told he might catch the plague. Well he might, but he might not. And if he did – what was the remedy?

As it began to grow light, he rose and washed himself thoroughly. This early, there was no problem throwing the dirty water from the window. He changed his clothes; the ones he'd been wearing stank of wine, meat and fat. They were greasy and stained. He shuddered when he thought of his exhibition the last evening. He threw the soiled clothing into a pile in a corner; let the servants deal with them. From the third of his three rooms he selected suitable day clothes. This room had been set up as a dressing room. Clothing and underwear filled the chests, with the surplus laid on the surfaces.

Cadd had barely completed changing when he was called. This was the day of the tests and, it became at once clear, they were to begin early. At six a.m. Why so untimely, he enquired of the servant as he pulled on his boots. And was told the King did not approve of Princes who 'lie abed'.

He followed the servant out into the courtyard. He had taken his cane as evidently there would be some walking; he hoped not too much. The castle was beginning to wake. There were servants scurrying about with firewood and buckets of water, though he saw no nobility at this hour. He and the servant left by a side gate of the castle and were shortly in the countryside. Mist lay in the hollows and caught in the trees. The sun was orange in the haze. He thought this would be the time to escape, but he was unprepared and had a servant with him. And so he followed on, into royal parkland.

There he found the other two princes, far less awake than he was – as he'd washed and changed while they still wore the greasy clothes from the meat feast. Crumbs and stains clung to their finery. Their faces were bleary-eyed and creased with hangover. Each had a servant attending. The only other person there was the Judge. He was a tall, thin man, almost skeletal in the boniness of his fingers and taut head, quite elderly, dressed completely in black – cloak, felt hat, shirt and leggings. He introduced himself and explained he had been the King's schoolteacher.

Spectators had been invited for the tests, but none were present. No surprise, considering where they all had been the night before. And Cadd was glad for that. The fewer witnesses to his humiliation the better.

The Judge introduced the Princes to each other. There was Prince Adol of Hoik whom he'd already met. Though he was much taller standing up. He kept playing with his thin moustache, pulling the crumbs of last night's banquet out of it. His hair was dark brown, cut straight below the ears, in inverted cup fashion. And he kept rapidly blinking to keep his eyes open in the dawn light.

The other prince was Prince Murm of Cartroy; another place he'd not heard of. But Cadd kept that to himself. Murm was short and stout, his blond hair was thinning at the front, though down to his shoulders at the side and back. His face was red after the exhaustions of the night before, and his forehead and stomach were obviously troubling him.

The three princes shook hands. The Judge exhorted them to be honourable in the three tests, and all nodded their agreement. They could hardly do otherwise.

The Judge said, 'The rules are simple. All that counts is a win. To come second or third is of no account. ' He looked to all three of them. 'It is a win – or nothing. Is that clear? '

The three princes assented that it was.

'Then let us begin. '

Each contestant retained their servant to fetch and carry. And they walked together, servants behind, to the site of the first test: a horse race.

At the designated place, three horses were tied to a tree. A groom was with them. The Princes drew straws. The longest had first selection, the middle next and the shortest last. Cadd drew the middle and pointed out a horse. It looked little different from the other two.

He had difficulty mounting. He had only ever ridden one horse. And this one was less forgiving. But eventually he got on top. And was able to follow the other two to the place where the race would start. On the way, Cadd tried to learn the ways of the horse. He had difficulty getting the animal to trot. Instead, it went straight into a canter – and then he had problems bringing the animal to a halt.

The race began with a wave of the groom's handkerchief, the Judge having made his way to the finish. And Cadd was left at the line. The horse reared and played him up. When he was at last able to get the horse to start – he had too much to make up. The others were well away. Cadd concentrated on riding; there was no glory left, he must simply finish. His horse went to a trot, then to a canter and a gallop – at which Cadd could merely hang on, while way ahead were the two galloping horses, where the real race was taking place. The course was half a mile. And when he arrived at the chestnut tree which was the winning post, the two princes had already dismounted. He had no idea who had won until he was told it was Prince Adol. Cadd dismounted and shook the Prince's hand.

'Well done,' he said.

'Just had the best horse,' said Adol modestly tweaking his moustache.

Without further ado, they were led to the site of the next test. This was archery. And for Cadd, this went even worse than the race. He had never in his life used a bow. They drew straws for bows. Cadd won, but it was no help to him as he had no idea what he was looking for – and simply picked one of the three at random.

The targets were large circles on easels about thirty yards away. Each was covered in fabric with three concentric rings, the inner being the bulls-eye. As Cadd had chosen first he was the last to shoot his three arrows which at least gave him the opportunity of watching the other two.

Prince Adol went first. He was obviously practised and got an arrow in each of the three rings – which didn't please him at all. Prince Murm went next. His first two arrows went in the middle of the three rings, and then his last went into the bull. He was triumphant and did a little dance of joy – for which he was admonished by the Judge.

Cadd took his turn. The string was harder to pull than he realised. And the first arrow did not make it far enough, and plopped into the ground about halfway to the target. He compensated with the second, and the arrow went over the top of it. And he did not bother with the third as he had already lost. So why make more of it?

He shook hands with Prince Murm.

'Well done,' he said.

'Beginner's luck,' beamed Murm.

They were led off to the third test. Cadd wondered what this third humiliation would be. In each test he had performed worse. Behind him, he could hear the other two talking. His ears were burning, though he couldn't hear their mumbling. Were they talking about him? His poor riding, his awful archery. And he was supposed to be competing for a princess. Perhaps he'd best resign and go for a scullery maid.

A wave of misery ran through him as he contemplated his situation. Soon it would all be over for him. He'd have nothing to do but leave, and return to the Prince having failed in his mission. His parents would then be executed, and it would be no surprise if he were to follow.

He wasn't even making a contest of it. Horse riding and archery – this was so unfair. It was as if whoever had chosen the tests was purposely laughing at him. So what princely skill would the third be? He suspected something like sword fighting which, never having tried it, he'd be hopeless at. These princes had instructors, had nothing better to do than fence and ride and shoot arrows – while he cleaned ovens. And that was a most unlikely test.

And he was right: it wasn't cleaning ovens. But neither was it sword fighting.

They were taken to a pool where a servant awaited them. They were instructed to strip to the waist and remove their boots. The servants took their clothing and soon all three princes were shivering in their leggings. Cadd was self-consciously aware of his stump. He left it in its sock, but it was obvious enough as he had difficulty standing. His stick was some support but he had to rest the stump on his foot.

The two princes and the Judge were trying hard not to look. But it was out: Prince Grude couldn't ride or shoot a bow – and had only one foot. Hardly a princess's choice.

The Judge said to the servant, 'Show them.'

The servant unwrapped a small cloth, and revealed a gold ring with a large red stone.

'That is the Princess's ring,' said the Judge. 'It is her favourite, given to her by her mother.' The Judge nodded to the servant. 'Now.'

At which the servant threw the ring far out into the pool.

'You must dive for it and bring it back,' said the Judge. 'Begin.'

The three of them crept tentatively into the water. Cadd retained his stick and had to hop. It was warmer than Cadd thought it would be. As the three stepped further in, rapidly the water became deep and was soon up to their waists. The two princes ahead of him had their arms raised out of the pond. Murm began to rub himself down with water, and dived flat out and began to swim. Adol followed suit. Cadd threw his stick back to the shore, and not wanting to be left out, took to swimming in their wake. None of them were good swimmers and they splashed along at roughly the same pace. Murm stopped, treading water; the others caught him up.

'About here,' he said.

The others agreed.

And the dive began. It was deep, surprisingly so, perhaps ten feet. And colder as Cadd struck lower. Had his gift survived his troubling last weeks? Was it lasting magic? Or something for the occasion?

Quickly, Cadd realised it was still with him. Although cold, he was not struggling for air. He could still breathe underwater. And he remembered his first talk with Bild on the carriage. Had the dwarf had some part in choosing this activity?

All three had reached the bottom, and were searching the mud. He could just make out their swollen cheeks, their legs pulling upwards as they came and went as if in a deep green fog. Suddenly Prince Adol gave him a look of alarm and shot to the surface, followed a few seconds later by Prince Murm. The urgency of their rise demonstrating their necessity for air.

Cadd continued searching. If the ring had actually sunk into the mud, then his gift might be no assistance. He could search for a week in this gloom. Here underwater, he was unsure where it had come down. Would the others come back? They were exhausted and still had to get back to shore. It hardly mattered if they did or didn't. He must find the ring.

He swam as close as he could to the bottom, his eyes inches away. He thought it wouldn't be lack of air that caused him to surface – but the cold. It was like being out on a winter's day, naked. His teeth chattered, his fingers were numbing. Another minute or two and he'd have to surface himself, just to warm up. A large trout came close by, investigated him, and swam in a sweeping curve through his legs.

And then he found the ring. The stone was uppermost, the glint of it catching his eye. He held it in the palm of his hand, put his eye close to make sure. And then pushed up to the surface.

He swam ashore and did not reveal the ring all at once. Servants closed in on him with towels, and swaddled him. A chair had appeared from somewhere and he was sat in it, for which he was at once grateful.

'We thought you were dead,' said the Judge anxiously.

'Drowned,' added Murm by way of unnecessary explanation.

Cadd smiled and revealed the ring.

The Judge had a close look at it, and agreed it was indeed the Princess's.

Murm shook Cadd's hand. 'Well done,' he said cheerlessly.

'Beginner's luck,' said Cadd.

The Judge consulted his notebook. He pursed his lips, and at last said, 'The tests have not been decisive. I see you have each won a contest. You the riding, Prince Adol. You the archery, Prince Murm. And you the diving, Prince Grude.' He put away his notebook and sighed. 'My part is over. It must now come to the choice of the Princess herself.'

Chapter 27

Cadd returned to his room. He ordered the servant to bring him a hot drink. And he removed the wet leggings, wiped himself down – and dressed once more. He lay out on a sofa; the day seemed old but it was barely past 8 a.m. And he sipped the hot blackcurrant. There was some time before his audience with the Princess. He would have liked to have slept, but it was not possible with the remnants of his hangover intermingling with the excitement of the occasion.

He had never seen the Princess. She had not come to greet him when he first arrived, she was not at the banquet, she was not at the tests. This was remarkable. In a little while he was to meet her for an hour or so – and in that time she must decide whether she wanted to marry him. Though if she did decide he was the one, it would not be Cadd whom she got. In fact, he reflected, it was to the real Prince's advantage that the interview was short. Cadd had come to do the courting for him. And he still had a one in three chance. Should he succeed – then the Prince would come for the marrying. And the Princess would know so little about him that she would have no inkling of the deception.

Should he succeed.

How odd that she had so little curiosity about her future husband. And suppose, say, Murm had won all three contests, then she would have had no choice at all – as it must be him as the overall winner. Suddenly it came to Cadd. They had all three won a test. It had been set up that way. He clapped his hands. How clever! The dwarf, he surmised, had brought all three princes in, and had asked each of them what they were especially good at. And that event was made one of the tests. He almost fell in love with the Princess at the thought of her intelligence. But then, why have three tests at all? After all, if they were all to win one – why bother competing, especially if she were not there to watch?

Her father! Of course. He wanted the tests. Cadd could imagine her going to him with the three contests: riding, archery and diving – and the King agreeing they were manly and princely.

But while the King wanted a winner, she wanted a choice of three. And the clever lady had got them.

She was interviewing them in order of the contest they had won. So Adol was first as winner of the riding, Murm second as winner of the archery, and he last as winner of the diving. Adol being first was at a disadvantage, as he had to go at once, still in his soiled clothes from the feast and with wet leggings. But maybe not, thought Cadd; perhaps she'd be sympathetic – and the discomfort might humanise the plodder.

Murm was at no disadvantage; he had an hour to change. And Cadd, more than enough time. So what was she like? Yes, clever. And Bild said she was beautiful. The combination Cadd found terrifying. A beautiful, intelligent Princess – that he was to woo – and win – or his parents would die.

This was a contest indeed.

What should he say to her? How should he act? He wished he had asked Bild. Should he be humble and compliant? Or should he be proud and arrogant, almost to the point of rudeness? What on earth did she want?

Of course, there was no way Cadd could know, but that didn't stop him imagining her in different ways. Haughty and cold, sweet and well-mannered – but what should he be? Was it like and like? Or was it that opposites attracted?

He had no experience at all in this business. And, he reflected, neither had Prince Grude. That's why he'd been sent in his place. The Prince didn't want to go a-wooing, especially if the lady could say no.

And she must say it twice.

Would she say it at the time? *I am sorry, Prince Grude, but I don't think you would make me a suitable husband. Have a safe journey home.*

Or would she say something non-committal: *Thank you for a delightful interview, Prince Grude. Rarely have I had a more entertaining time. I shall send you my decision this afternoon.*

And he would kiss her hand and leave, thinking he was in with the best of chances, only to receive the rejection, short and polite, late afternoon.

Cadd paced his room, inventing scenes, rejecting them, trying another, speaking his lines out loud in varying tones, words of love, of pride, poetic, masterful – and then their opposites. Or would her beauty and intelligence simply strike him dumb – and he be hard pressed to mumble even yes or no?

By the time the servant came for him, he wished he, too, could have a deputy.

Chapter 28

The servant led him across the courtyard, and into another building, within the castle, where the Princess' chambers lay. The servant knocked at the door, and when invited to enter, introduced Prince Grude, bowed and then left.

The Princess stepped forward to greet him. She was utterly unlike the Princess of his imagination. She was short, perhaps five inches shorter than he was. She had a pretty face, with long, brown, straight hair down to her waist. A thick golden band held it back off her forehead. She wore a bright yellow dress, bare at the shoulders, down to her ankles, below which could be seen soft green shoes. And she had a hunchback. There was no attempt to disguise it. Her back was curved with a round bump, just below the shoulders.

Cadd took her hand, bowed and kissed it. He had been taught this was the correct greeting.

'I am pleased to meet you, Your Highness.'

The bow allowed him to remove his expression of surprise on first seeing her. Though he suspected she had noticed.

She smiled at him. 'I think we may dispense with the Your Highness,' she said. 'We are of the same rank. I am Rosalie.'

'I am honoured to meet you, Rosalie.'

'And I you, Grude.'

She curtseyed lightly, turned and gestured him to sit on the sofa with her. Her sitting room was large and well lit, with long windows draped from floor to ceiling. There were flowers in the various vases on the chests about the room. And here and there, dolls, male and female, some seated, some standing, some in little groups. An embroidery in a frame was lying on a table by the window and next to it a book, open face down.

Cadd made his way to join her on the sofa.

'I see you have a stick,' she said, already seated.

'I was born with only one foot,' said Cadd, keeping his story straight.

'And I with this.' She patted her back and smiled at him.

The sofa was long, and so there was no danger of them accidentally touching. On a low table before them were cakes, fruit and cordial.

'May I offer you a drink?' she said.

Cadd accepted a lemon drink. He refused the cake, thinking he could not handle it and speak.

She said, 'Excuse me if I don't join you – but this is my third interview this morning.'

'I think you arranged it that way,' said Cadd.

'What do you mean?' she said sharply.

Cadd wished he hadn't made his careless remark but it was too late now.

'I think the tests were set up for us all to win one.'

He was bristling at the neck. How might she take this?

She smiled, bringing out the dimples in her cheeks. 'I wondered whether you would discover me.' And when Cadd looked at her quizzically, she added, 'Bild has given me full reports on all of you.'

'Bild drove all three of us in?' he asked.

She nodded. 'And enquired of your strengths. My father was all for the three contests. So I had to go with him. But I wanted to see you all. Why should it be the best archer and the best horseman whom I marry? Are those good qualities for a husband?'

Cadd grinned. He could not agree more with her sentiments.

'And your mother,' he said. 'What did she have to say about it?'

She pursed her lips and was silent for a few seconds. Then said, 'My mother was not asked. I doubt that you know the situation. But I suppose I have to tell you...' She hesitated, then went on, 'There is no divorce in Witland. And my mother objected to my father's mistress. And so has been banished from court.'

She rose and walked about, rubbing her hands agitatedly.

'I don't always get on with my father,' she said. 'But I am his only heir. No matter how many bastards that woman has – short of assassination, I shall be Queen.' She looked hard at him. 'And I am sure that's why you are here.'

'My father...' he mumbled, 'he thought...' He could not go on.

She did it for him. 'He thought marry Princess Rosalie and we get Witland without losing a man.'

Cadd could see she was angry, and so did not answer. He sipped his lemon drink. She did not speak either, and he thought, I must say something.

'I was surprised not to see you at the banquet,' he said.

'I hate those meat circuses,' she said. 'Everyone gets drunk, and spits and curses and throws their food. And my father encourages it.' She sat down again. 'Besides,' she added, 'it's no place for a princess with a hunchback.'

Cadd could see that, imagining the remarks, the sniggering. He understood she would not allow herself to be a public spectacle. But here with her flowers and dolls, her drink and hospitality – she was in charge.

'Tell me about your parents,' she said.

Cadd faltered, then said, 'My father is a good man. Respected. He works hard, he cares for his family.'

'I'm glad of that,' said Rosalie. 'And your mother?'

'She works with him. Together they run things.'

Rosalie nodded as he spoke. 'Yes, that is the way to run a kingdom. Why should there just be a King with total power – and his Queen simply there to bear him sons? She should share the business of state.'

Cadd nodded. In reality he had been describing his own family. How his mother and father ran the bakery. Used to run the bakery. His eyes welled with tears. He tried to quell them, but it was useless and they filled his eyes.

'You must love them,' she said softly.

Cadd nodded. He was unable to speak.

'But you have only been away from them a little while,' she said. 'Why do you weep?'

'There... have been troubles,' he managed to say, thinking quickly. What troubles? 'My brothers have been killed in battle.'

'I am so sorry,' she said.

They were quiet for a little while.

'I am an only child,' she said. 'A girl at that. What could be worse! That's why my father devised the tests. He wants a son-in-law who will be a son to him. A champion who can ride and shoot, and hack off heads in battle.'

'And you want someone a little quieter,' said Cadd.

'I don't give a damn whether he can ride or shoot a bow. What's the army for?' She turned to face Cadd. 'I want someone who can love me.'

Cadd blushed and looked away. And when he glanced back a little later he noted that she too had reddened.

'My father wants me to marry you,' he said.

'But do you want to marry me?'

'I think...' he began, halted, and said firmly: 'Yes.' Made easier as he wasn't saying it for himself, though on consideration he thought – she wouldn't be so bad.

'Are you sure of that?'

She was looking searchingly into his eyes. And so he looked into hers, as he must – as to falter would deny his words.

'I am,' he said.

She grinned. 'Bild said you were the best of the three. And he's usually right. You are so unlike the other two. I talked with Murm about hunting for an hour. He did not even notice I was bored silly after ten minutes… Adol kept asking me about my father's castles. He knew them all better than me.'

Cadd laughed. 'You're nothing like I thought you would be.'

'Good,' she said and kissed him on the forehead. 'That's for my future husband.'

Cadd could scarcely believe it. He was there. Mission accomplished. And yet he was saddened. He liked Rosalie, and would have to hand her over to the Prince. That was the power of princes over bakers' boys.

'Do you mind,' he said, 'if I take off my boot?'

'Be my guest,' she said.

He removed both boots, though it was only his stump boot that was bothering him. He removed the sock from it.

'It's very red,' she said.

'I've had a hard morning. Riding, archery, diving – and all that walking between. And last night's banquet didn't do it much good.' He rubbed the pink flesh, then held up the stump for her to view. 'Take a good look. Now – do you still want to marry me?'

She pursed her lips and fingered the tip. 'Shall I show you my hump?'

He wasn't sure whether or not she was serious, and so did not reply.

She laughed and rang a little bell on the table beside her. In a few seconds a maid came running in. She curtseyed before her mistress.

'Your Highness?'

'Bring me warm water, mustard and rosemary.'

The maid left.

Rosalie turned to him. 'When my back hurts, I bathe it in mustard and rosemary…'

'Does it hurt now?' he said, puzzled and a little embarrassed.

'I thought it might work on your stump,' she said. 'And as we are to be betrothed, I think you might massage my back for me.' She turned. 'Please.'

Cadd placed his hands on her hump. 'Here?'

'Yes – and be firm.'

He began tentatively, and then thought it reminded him of warm dough, and was more vigorous.

'Oh that's very pleasant,' she sighed, wriggling her back. 'You must have other young ladies with hunchbacks.'

'One only.' Her back was warm and soft under his hands as he massaged her down from the shoulders, over her hump to her waist. And then began upwards once more, both hands traversing together. He stopped over her hump and could feel the beat of her heart through it. And wondered what the hump was like under her dress. Had she been serious when she said he might see it? But no. That was not a question he dare put to a princess.

'If I had any doubts,' she murmured, 'I don't have them now.'

'But you might have had a racer or an archer?' he said, smoothing his hands across her shoulders.

'I would rather have a diver,' she whispered.

The maid entered with a bowl of water, a dish of mustard and some sprigs of rosemary. Cadd felt somewhat compromised as there was no disguising what he was doing.

But the Princess merely smiled and said, 'Thank you, Giza – that will be all.'

The maid curtseyed and left.

'My turn,' said the Princess. She did a half twist and took his wrists. 'Sit down, please.'

She released his arms and he sat down and watched her as she knelt on the carpet and put her hand into the bowl of water. 'Good,' she said. Then poured in a little mustard and stirred the water around, watching the spinning water like a mesmerised child. Unsatisfied, she added a little more mustard, then the rosemary.

'Your stump please.'

He presented it to her. And she bathed it in the warm balm, rubbing it over the red, swollen end with her extended fingers as if she were moulding a pot.

'We are the perfect couple,' she said.

'We are,' he agreed.

And knew it was true. He'd said his words of love earlier as part of his mission. But he was no longer on a mission. It was simple – he loved her. That girl on the ground, bathing his stump. It was so simple, it was what he needed. He had been abused, thrown around, chained up – and these gentle hands at last freed him.

'When we are married, you will bathe me,' she said, looking up from her task.

'Yes,' he said, gazing into the depths of her eyes.

He stretched out with both hands and held her head, his fingers tangled in her hair. She twisted a little and kissed his fingers.

'Oh,' she exclaimed, 'I want to marry you.'

She sighed, slowly rose and shook herself. 'I am a princess. You are a prince. We must do this properly, my love.'

He nodded reluctantly.

'I will tell my father straight away. You must send a messenger to yours.'

It was only then that Cadd thought – what have I done? What have I done to Princess Rosalie? Married this beautiful girl to Prince Grude. But he could not think that way, dare not – as he must make the most of his time with her. She was his, he was hers – that was all there was to think. The present held him. He could not think ahead.

She helped him put on his boots. At the door, they embraced.

'You shall be my husband. I know I have chosen the right one.'

And Cadd left in a rainbow of happiness.

Chapter 29

In the courtyard he walked into the warmth and light as if new born. As if all this was newly made for him alone. Cadd gazed into the blue of the sky. How could it be so blue? How far did it go? He could see no end to it. Did it know she loved him? Was it watching him watching it?

He looked around the courtyard, at its busyness. How could all this go on – did they not know the way he felt? Did they not realise the world had changed completely? Barrels were being rolled into a cellar, a woman was struggling with a pail of water while another was pulling at the pump to fill hers. Straw was being taken off a wagon by two men; the horse had its head in a bucket. How were they able to carry on?

'How did it go?'

Cadd was surprised by the interruption, and turned to the speaker who was behind him. It was Prince Adol, now cleaned up and tweaking his moustache. He was stretched out in a chair, a footstool under his feet. A servant stood behind him, and another two were on the ground on cushions.

Cadd beamed at him. 'Quite well, I think.' And added for politeness, 'And your own interview?'

Adol beamed back. 'Brilliant. I thought it might go so badly. I had to go at once and so was still in my dirty clothes...' He stopped to take in a satisfied breath. 'But once we got on to castles – it was as if a fire had started. You know her father has nine? Of course you do. We discussed them as living spaces, as defence, as prestige, as ornaments of architecture... I couldn't get her off the subject. She loves castles as much as I do.'

Cadd could not stop grinning. It was as if his whole body was a cauldon of happiness and the grin must bubble out of him.

'We didn't talk about castles,' he said.

Adol clicked his tongue. 'Tt-tt. You missed an opportunity.'

'How's Murm?' said Cadd.

Adol sighed. 'Poor chap. The girl mesmerised him and he could hardly say a word. He's packing at the moment. Says he wants to be away as quickly as possible.' He stopped and opened his hands. 'What can I say? He had his chance. I went in smelling like a stable – and made the most of things.'

'Did she agree to marry you?'

'Not in so many words, but a man can tell. The glances, the smiles. She was sighing all the time... and what was that – if not love?'

Cadd knew of another possibility but instead held out his hand.

'Congratulations.'

Adol took his hand. 'Thank you, my fine fellow. This is sporting of you. You must come to visit us after we are married.'

'I should love to see your castles,' said Cadd.

'You shall. You shall! I shall take you round personally...' He stopped, 'Might I say something, dear chap, please don't take this wrongly...' He pressed his fingers to his lips as if to select the right words. 'I have noted you wander about without servants... A word to the wise, it has been noted. It is not seemly, Grude. It is not Princely. Who are we if we simply wander alone?'

'A prince must be seen to be a prince.'

Adol slapped his thigh. 'Exactly.' He leaned forward and said quietly, 'It reflects on the rest of us if you remove the show.'

'I shall try harder,' said Cadd.

'Good fellow.' And he lay back, eyes closed, the sun shining on his face.

And Cadd walked away, knowing exactly whom he was when he wandered alone. He had seen it in her eyes. Adol was a nice chap, but all he could see were castles and show. And could not see it meant nothing. Even now – who were these people bowing and curtseying to? It wasn't to Cadd crossing the courtyard, but to some show, someone they thought he was – but he wasn't at all.

Drawn by the breeze, he strolled out of the main gate and stood on the drawbridge looking into the moat. Three swans were sailing towards him in a stately flotilla. They at least knew, as did the dancing light on the water, bursting like the happiness popping within him. He was loved. He loved. Everything was changed. His fingers stroked the chain of the drawbridge, in and around the rough links. It was if he'd never felt iron before. He was a link, linked to all and everyone. Why could the guard at the bridge not see it? Why could that downcast man with a sack over his back not see it? Was he simply thinking of dumping his burden and his next meal?

We are links!

Cadd remained a while contemplating the water. The fluid that has no joins, he thought. The impossible beauty of the light carries the ripples. He had to move at last when Murm came through on horseback with a few servants behind.

'Goodbye,' said Murm curtly.

Cadd said, 'I'm sorry it didn't go well for you.'

'I made a fool of myself,' said the Prince and kicked his horse to a trot.

Cadd watched him and his servants ride to the camp of soldiers along the walls. He wondered that anyone could be so unhappy on such a beautiful day. And took himself, step by amazing step, back over the drawbridge and into the castle where his love lived.

Chapter 30

He would write a poem to Rosalie. It would have three swans and the bluest sky in it. It would have the feeling of her fingers on the bruising where his leg ended. And a busy courtyard that did not know there was a new love in the world.

Cadd opened the door of his chambers, his head in verse. And was at once grabbed by the arms and shoulders and pulled into the room. The door was slammed behind him. It was so quick, he was so unprepared, that he could not resist. Though it would have been useless.

Two soldiers held him; a third had closed the door. And before him stood Loo with a dagger which he now pressed to Cadd's throat.

'Well, here's a prince back from wooing. I would love to cut your throat – but we are guests here – and mustn't stain the carpet.'

He gave Cadd a push. 'Tie his hands.'

Cadd's hands were pulled behind his back. Loo's pale face was in shadow against the light, as if all colour had been extracted and gone into his blond hair.

Cadd winced as the bonds were pulled tight.

'You have done well, baker's boy. You could give us all lessons in love. The word is already about that Prince Grude and Princess Rosalie are to be betrothed. You have been a wonderful double.'

'What do you want with me?' said Cadd, his hands swelling at the tightness of the rope.

'You have completed your mission,' said Loo. 'And we have no further use for you.'

'But the Prince... surely he...?'

'No,' said Loo. 'One task. Fulfilled. And one double who must be disposed of.'

'But the King knows I'm here,' he tried desperately. 'The Princess…'

Loo waved a hand disdainfully. 'Petty matters. A messenger has just arrived saying that your father is ill. You must leave at once.' Loo laughed. 'And we are your leaving party.'

Cadd looked at the steely blue eyes, the pitiless face. There would be no mercy.

'In a week,' went on Loo, 'the Prince will return to claim his betrothed and to make preparations for the wedding…' Loo blew into his face. 'Don't you see, my young mudfish – there cannot be two Princes here. One alone, to claim the prize. You have done well for a baker's boy. Met the King of Witland. Had some good food at his table. Been bowed and curtseyed to by all and sundry… Many would give their life for that.'

'Was this always the plan?' said Cadd.

'Of course.'

'What of my family? Are they alive?'

'I know nothing of your family.'

Cadd was overwhelmed. Such deceit; to die as soon as he had succeeded. Surely not?

'Has the Prince no gratitude?'

'None.'

'Suppose I had failed?'

Loo laughed. 'A bad servant deserves death.'

'And a good one?'

Loo widened his eyes. 'Must be killed before he makes a mistake.' Loo tapped Cadd on the nose with the flat of the knife. 'We are simply protecting your reputation.'

Cadd's mouth was dry. What was there to say? It was well thought out. He was to be murdered – and his absence excused by the Prince's father's sudden illness. Which would heal quickly. And then the Prince would return to claim his bride.

But they couldn't kill him here. Loo had already said that. They couldn't leave a dead Prince in his chambers. How could he then rise up to marry?

'Gag him.'

A scarf was tied round his mouth.

Loo pressed the dagger to Cadd's neck. 'I would kill you here, mudfish. Soldiers are always impatient. But they tell me waiting is succulent. So I shall place this sweet pear upon a dish until it grows juicy and ripe. And then I shall cut it in quarters and eat it.' He snapped his finger. 'Put him in the sack.'

A flour sack was thrust over Cadd's head, making him sneeze as the dust went up his nose. The fabric was pulled down over his body, his legs pushed in – and the end tied up.

He was now blind baggage, but could hear the instructions of the men in the room. Loo ordered them to empty a chest. Were they going to bury him alive? Loo would go for a slow, lingering death, of that he was sure.

He was almost choking with the flour dust as he was lifted by head and feet, his throat burning. In a paroxysm of coughing, he was dropped into the chest, his head thrust down and the lid slammed. In darkness, he was carried away.

Chapter 31

He could tell by the swaying and creaking that he was on a wagon. There was the clip of the horses, voices – he couldn't make out the words. But barely cared, as his discomfort was excruciating. The confines and tightness of the sack forced his knees against his chest. His feet were unbound but that mattered little as he couldn't move them at all. He was lying on his hands, hurting his back and crushing his wrists. He'd spent the last hour or so straining at the ropes in order to make some slack – but had no success. The soldiers knew well how to bind a prisoner so he stayed bound.

They would be the Prince's soldiers heading back, he knew. On the way they would kill him, once safely away from the castle. And bury him deep. While Rosalie, who was already telling the world of her impending betrothal, had been informed he had rushed away to see his sick father. And she would wait, without suspicion, for his return in a week.

Not so long to wait for your love.

He'd been a fool. Thought Loo had little power. But once Cadd's mission was achieved then it was Loo who had all the power. It was he who had none. And a bigger fool, to believe the Prince; to think he would have many tasks for him. Doubles are dangerous. And now the Prince had taken Tolga, he could take his Princess too.

Were his parents alive? The messenger who had come earlier had said they had been spared. But why, if Grude intended killing him? Perhaps just playing his options. They'd been a useful tool. Easily disposed of at any time.

And all the time Loo had been scheming and waiting. What a fool Cadd had been! He was important until Rosalie had been wooed – and then as disposable as this flour sack, once the flour was in the bin. He might be the Prince's double but he could not match him in ruthlessness. Death, he had known, might well be his end, but it had not crossed his mind that he had but one task to fulfil – and the reward would be so swift.

Might the Prince kill Loo? For his knowledge of the deception. Might he kill everyone on this detachment? So what if he did? It would be of no help to Cadd. No help to Rosalie who would marry the Prince. Deceived by Cadd, led to misery by her love.

He wept. For the pain of being trussed like a chicken in this choking sack, for his pending death and for the life in death that his love must lead. Loo was right. He was a baker's boy. Chosen because he was wrongly thought to be the fourth son of a fourth son of a baker. With a baker's boy's hopes and a baker's boy's dreams. All his efforts had been useless. Worse than useless. His town had been sacked, everyone killed. His parents spared temporarily, but that would soon be remedied. A few hours ago he had found love – and that was to be annihilated too. Would Rosalie even know that Grude was not the one who had wooed her? Or would she believe she had erred? And live to regret it until she died.

Pity any woman who married Grude. Pity any baker's boy who was his double.

But there was no one to pity them. His parents and Jel would need it for themselves. His other brothers, killed on the battlefield. Rosalie, happily awaiting his return. No pity from Loo or his men. They would dig a hole and drop him in it. And pile the earth on top and stamp it down. While he could not raise a finger.

Sooner ask the cat to pity the mouse in its claws.

Then let it come in haste. He had been near death so many times these past weeks that he was not frightened of it. A long dying, he dreaded. But not death. When all you love are dead, but one. And what could he do for her? Except give his apologies to the walls of the sack. Tell it he hadn't known.

Only he had. She was the sacrifice to get his family back.

He could claim he would have told her. But he hadn't. And could he have done? Wasn't it a condition, so he believed, that she must marry the Prince to secure the release of his family? It was. It was. There was no need to lie to himself.

Death – come quickly.

Chapter 32

The wagon halted. There was a barking of orders, movement, the neighing of horses. In his dark confines he tried to imagine what was going on. Were they making camp? Or was this the place for him? The final one.

The chest was lifted. He could hear the intakes of breath, the complaining of the weight. First upwards, a shaking halt, then rapidly down with a bump that shook his bones. He guessed he'd been taken off the wagon and was now on the ground.

And there he stayed, with activity all around. This couldn't last, he knew there was a plan for him which was being prepared. Were they digging? He couldn't hear shovels – but need they be so close? He had a sudden dread. Might they be lighting a fire? Oh, that would remove all evidence of a failed prince.

He was a mass of pain; the hours in the chest, rolled up like a mattress, the dust in his throat, his crushed and bloated hands – and the thoughts of death and the pain he had brought to others. It would come to an end soon.

He welcomed it.

And yet – a small voice cried out to live. That fool of a voice; no doubt it had cried out in the breasts of his brothers on the battlefield, in his townsfolk as their doors were smashed in… The urge to survive. In every worm and beetle as the boot comes down.

Let it come quick.

The lid was opened. Pricks of light entered the sack. It was still daylight then on this long, long day. Hands came at either end of him. They had some trouble pulling him out, as he was so jammed in. Realising they couldn't do it together, they jerked his legs violently. His head struck the bottom of the chest, then he was drawn along by the legs, clumsily lifted and scraped over the edge. And dropped like a sack of potatoes.

This was the worst of it. The knowing. The cow entering the slaughterhouse doesn't know its throat is about to be cut. But he'd known since he had opened the door of his chamber and saw Loo. The sour captain who had wanted to kill him since those first hours at camp – and would have done but for the entrance of the Prince into his life. Loo, whom Cadd had sent to bed without supper like a naughty schoolboy. Loo, who enjoyed his revenge taken hot – was now to take it at the very boil.

The neck of the sack was untied. Cadd groaned as his stiff legs fell into new space. He was kicked in the ribs.

'Does he think we are going to free him, lads?' exclaimed Loo. 'What do you think – shall we let him go?'

Laughter all round.

Cadd had nothing to say. Could say nothing, gagged.

'This copy,' said Loo, with a kick. 'This impostor.' Kick. 'This shadow.' Kick. 'This snivelling deputy.' Kick. 'Dared to believe he was the Prince. This battered baker's boy who had the luck of being a double...' Kick to the ribs, head, back. 'Gave orders like one, sat at the top table with the King, wooed the Princess...' Kick, kick, kick. 'And died like a rabbit in a gin.'

Cadd was bleeding and bruised. He could not evade the kicks, nor cry out for them to stop. Wherever he was – there was no help. He was at their mercy. And they had none.

Let it come quick.

The sack end was opened wider; stones and rocks were thrown in, pushed in further until he felt almost buried in the bag. His legs were forced back in and the end was retied. Crushed, barely conscious, in half-painful sleep. Release from pain was all he wanted.

And now – lifted. There must be four or five heaving this bag of rock and bones. And rested. He was on a wall, rocks pressing into his back, bruises stinging down his body.

'Let him go,' yelled Loo.

Hands rolled him over an edge, and he was in free fall. Rock, body and sack falling together...

Splash!

Chapter 33

He lay on the bottom. How deep – twelve, fifteen feet, estimating from how long it took him to hit the mud. Icy cold, but at last free of them. They must have gone, given him five minutes to make sure – and then ridden off to Larken to collect their Prince.

For the first time in hours, he realised he could survive. He was out of Loo's domain. And he could breathe under water. Though if he could not free himself soon he would die of the cold. The stones held him down, otherwise his body might float up and, if not too bloated, still be recognised. Another prince, to complicate matters for the living one.

He must get out of the sack.

He squirmed and wriggled until there were rocks underneath him, then pushed and pulled until he could turn sideways in the tight sacking. Behind his back, his swollen fingers felt the stones. Tried this one, that one. And found a stone with a sharp edge. He had no hope in cutting the ropes but if he could rip the sack...

It was difficult to grasp it. His fingers were so painful, he had so little room. But holding it as well as he could, he pressed it against the fabric, exasperated that he could apply so little pressure. Up and down, he sawed the fabric with the sharp edge. He could barely feel the stone, his puffed-up fingers were now so numb – and in a short while with the cold and tightness they would not be able to grip at all.

He must get out of the sack. Or die within.

Determination had taken over. He'd pitied himself enough. He must live now, not die like a dog in a river. Feverishly he sawed, willing the fibres to tear.

And suddenly there was give. Perhaps half an inch, the smallest of rips. He pressed at it with the rock, hoping to push it through and enlarge the hole, but his hands were too feeble. He wriggled and squirmed and thrust at the sacking with his boots, his knees, his head and back.

And the rip grew. Behind his back, he was able to put his bound hands through. Then tried tearing at the sides but his hands were too weak. If he could get his feet in the hole – but they were too far off. And he was too crushed to bring them round.

He desperately pushed and kicked where he could. Pressed and stretched at every point of contact. Both boots, head and back and arms forcing at the fabric, straining every muscle to break out of the bag.

And it gave.

His arms were out of the sack, up to the shoulders. If he could move so as to get his head through, he might be able to get out. With great effort he rolled over, abrading his body on the stones. But once on his front, his head couldn't get to the hole. Frantically, he pushed and stretched. Twisted his head, here and there – what limited motion he had. And there was the hole. Nearly, nearly... And his nose was out. He must bring his forehead down that few inches. He thrust and squirmed, and suddenly, like a baby being born, his head burst through.

And took with it his shoulders. From there, it was easy. Chest, hips and legs eased out of their womb, and he entered the world once more.

The water was murky, with a glow of greenish light filtering down from the top. Though his arms were bound and his mouth still gagged, his legs were unfettered. Kicking gently, as he could do no more, he slowly rose to the surface.

At the top, he lay on his back exhausted, but knew there could be no rest or he would die of cold. He must get to the shore. Too weak to swim across the current, he went with the flow, making a slight angle to the bank. He gave himself small goals: swim until level with that tree. Then rest to a count of ten. To that bush... To that rock.

Until his feet found the muddy bottom – and he was able to stand. Shaky and shivering, weaker than a grass stalk, he plodded to the beach. And collapsed on the stones, gasping like a flounder on a slab.

Chapter 34

Cadd was able to remove the gag by rubbing at the rough bark of a tree trunk. It hung knotted round his neck, like the scarf it was. He could do nothing with the ropes around his wrists. If anything, they were tighter, the water having swollen the rope strands. He made some attempts to drag his feet through his bound hands, so he could get them in front of him. But the binding was too tight. He lacked the suppleness – and was simply too tired.

He must get help.

Cadd staggered along the river bank. A light breeze chilled his bones. He could not feel his hands. They could go black and rot, he knew, once they lost their blood supply. How long did he have?

The sun was low in the sky. It would be dark in an hour. He shivered in his wet clothes, but couldn't get them off to wring them. And how anyway? He shuffled from foot to foot. Stopped, rested, would have rested longer but knew it would be harder to find help after nightfall.

He did not want to lose his hands.

Cadd rounded a bend. And saw a man in a field, head bowed as he pushed a small wooden plough.

'Sir!' called Cadd.

The man did not look up; Cadd's voice was too feeble. So he stumbled onto the field.

'Sir! Sir!' he called hoarsely as he trod the furrows.

The man had his back to him, ploughing away from Cadd, so he was losing ground on him. But then the man swung round, evidently at the end of his strip – and saw Cadd making his way towards him. The man stopped and waited, wondering at the odd gait of the stranger and why his hands should be behind his back.

Cadd fell between furrows, and pulled himself up – at which the man, sensing a problem, began heading towards Cadd. He stumbled a few steps further, then waited.

The ploughman approached. He was middle-aged with greying hair, wearing a rough sleeveless tunic to his knees. His grizzled face had a look of puzzlement, as he still had not grasped the situation.

'Please, sir,' gasped Cadd. 'Help me.'

He rolled over and showed his bound wrists.

'Who did this?' exclaimed the man.

'Soldiers,' said Cadd. 'They tried to drown me.'

The man looked at him suspiciously. 'Whose soldiers?'

'From Larken.'

'Larken? What are they doing here?'

Cadd shook his head. He knew explanation was useless.

The man sighed, and took a knife from his belt. 'Funny games these soldiers play.'

Cadd tried to rise and fell back.

'Stay down,' said the man. And kneeled behind him to cut the bonds.

His knife wasn't sharp. Better at cutting apples and turnips than rope. But the man persevered and in a few minutes a key rope was severed. He untwisted the rope from Cadd's wrists.

With a yell of agony, Cadd swung his arms to the front.

'Thank you, thank you,' he couldn't stop saying as he thrust his wrists to his mouth and sucked the rope burns, licked at his fingers, while groaning in pain. He waved his hands in the breeze as if trying to dry them. Trying to throw off the pain and drive blood into them.

'You're done in, lad,' said the ploughman. 'You'd best come back with me.'

Chapter 35

Cadd fell when he tried to stand. His body had given up. Now there was help, it refused to struggle. The man, realising his state, left him and said he'd be back. Cadd lay out in the field, like a broken scarecrow. His teeth chattered; he was a mass of bruising, as weak as a bird fallen from the nest. Too tired to feel relief in escape. Too tired to do anything but lie facing the sky.

A while later, the man returned with a wheelbarrow. His wife was with him, a strong woman wearing a headscarf and a dress down to her ankles. The two of them lifted Cadd like a rag doll into the wheelbarrow, head to the fore, legs poking between the handles. The man pushed and the woman pulled from the front as the wheelbarrow bumped up and down the furrows of the field. Cadd was jostled like a bag of seed.

It was a timeless voyage, staring into the depths of the sky and the fringing treetops, bumped and lost and found again. A painful journey, without an ending. His hands might be free but they bore the memory of the binding. Bruised and exhausted, as he would always be.

At the door of a cottage, they stopped. The man and woman carried him inside. Three children were moved away from the fire as he was plumped down before it.

'He's soaking,' said the woman. 'He must get out of those wet things – or he'll never warm up.'

Together, they took off Cadd's clothes. He had no resistance. As they removed his jacket, the woman felt the embroidery and looked to her husband. He put a finger to his lips and she nodded. Evidently this was no ordinary traveller.

Once undressed, Cadd was wiped down with a cloth – and wrapped in a blanket. But it was not enough to warm him, and he shivered, although by the fire. The man brought him a smock and helped him put it on with some leggings. With these and the blanket on, at last he felt warmer.

Later, the woman brought him soup. He clutched the bowl in swollen hands and was for the first time aware of the whole family watching him; the three children, the man and the woman, the firelight flickering in their faces as the day eased into night.

'Thank you,' he said feebly. 'I'm most grateful.'

'Eat up,' said the woman. 'Don't talk.'

After the food, they put him to bed, not bothering to undress him. And he was asleep almost at once.

Cadd slept the night through.

When he woke in the morning, there was no-one in the cottage. The fire was smoking in the grate, mottled sunlight playing on the earth floor. Cadd lay back, refreshed enough to begin thinking what he must do. He felt in no immediate danger. Loo thought he was dead, and anyway was well on the way to Larken. This peasant family, though, must be puzzled at the guest who turns up out of the blue, hands bound, wearing rich clothing. Might they betray him?

Perhaps he should slip away. But he took no action on the thought. The heat of the bed was too comforting. And he was still exhausted after the efforts of the day before. The questions would come now; he knew it. He thought of the story he would tell the family, and in alarm he wondered – where were they now? Suppose they came back with the Lord of the Manor? He might fool a peasant family with a tale, but not a Lord who could question and counter-question.

A little later the family returned. The three children had been picking blackberries and each had a bowlful held carefully in two hands. The woman carried a bundle of sticks, and the man a bucket of water. Cadd thought: now it comes.

The man sat on the bed, a smile on his weather-beaten face. 'Feeling better, young 'un?'

'I am, thank you, sir.'

'That's good to hear.' The man came in closer, put a finger to his lips and indicated back at the children, before going on quietly. 'I don't know who you are. And it's better I don't know. It's plain you're in trouble; and you are no ordinary person. But if it please you, we'll shelter you for one more night – and then you must leave us.'

'I'm grateful for the help you have already given me, sir.'

The man grimaced. 'Don't mind that. But we're just ordinary folk. It's no good for us to get mixed up in gentlemen's quarrels.'

'I understand.'

'I have to think of my family.'

How could Cadd not understand? He was a dangerous person to hide. A Prince's double who had wooed a princess. Help him and you might easily lose your life – and your family's too. He was grateful though that the man didn't pry and force him to lie.

'I have buried your clothes,' said the man.

Cadd was surprised at his astuteness. 'Thank you,' he said.

A little later, he ate bread and cheese with the family and some blackberries. All washed down with weak beer. He wished he could talk to them, but to speak would be to invite questions, so he limited himself to praising the food. The father ushered them out for the afternoon's tasks. Cadd would have liked to have helped, but the man and woman insisted that he rest. And he gave in, knowing he couldn't be much help to them.

That afternoon, he sat outside the cottage on a pile of firewood. It was warm, with breezy autumn sunshine. A woodpecker was pecking at a nearby tree, and a hunting bird hovered over the fields. Yesterday he had fallen in love. Yesterday he'd been shut in a box. Yesterday he'd been brought back to life.

Decisions had to be made.

Except when it came to it, there were none to make. They were there already. There was no alternative. He knew what he must do.

He must go back to the castle.

Chapter 36

The next day Cadd was sent off. He had slept well again, but aware, now he was mending, that he was sleeping in the children's bed. The three of them had been relegated to a patch of straw in a corner. The night before he'd simply taken what he was given, but this second night he realised what an imposition he was. Not merely the danger that attended him, but the space he took from others. And he felt it was right to leave.

He thanked them profusely. So much so, that he saw that he was embarrassing the man – and stopped. But what else could he say?

The woman gave him some food for the journey. Neither asked where he was going.

'If we don't know, we can't tell,' said the man.

At the last minute the man gave him a briar stick and a hood. At first Cadd would not take them. He had had too much already. But the man insisted.

'You are to walk, lad. There'll be no wheelbarrow today. I can find another briar in the hedgerow. And I've hats enough.'

Cadd took them, wearing the hood round his neck, until he should need to pull it over his head. The stick was a stout one and he'd need it if he were to get to the castle. He wasn't too sure which direction it was, but couldn't ask without revealing his destination. Loo had been heading for Larken when he dropped Cadd in the river. So that meant he must go west – the direction the sun had set.

And which way was that?

The family waved him off, all of them at their cottage door seeing him away. And there they remained, until he turned a bend and they were gone from his life. Their kindness had warmed him. Given him hope. Made him believe there was not simply wickedness in the world.

Cadd had not walked more than half a mile when he was tired. He sat down and reasoned his direction. The sun was there. It had risen about there – so he must go in the opposite direction. More or less, he hoped. He rose reluctantly. It would take time for him to be able to walk any distance with one good foot, even in the best of health. He'd recovered somewhat after two nights of rest, but was stiff – and there was a weariness reluctant to leave his bones, insisting he rest every few hundred yards.

He paced himself, walking a while, resting, picking blackberries. After an hour or so, he stopped to bathe his foot in a stream. It was going to be a long, slow day. He hoped he'd make the castle by nightfall – but if it took longer, then it took longer. The stream crossed the roadway and he sat on a rock, eating bread and cheese and enjoying the ease of being alone.

His task was fixed inside him. It was simple. He must inform Princess Rosalie that she must not marry the Prince. The Prince was a beast – and simply wanted her for the kingdom that came with her. He would make her life a misery. How Cadd would explain his part in it, or rather how she would take his deception, he cared not to dwell on, hoping she would accept his contrition.

She might reward him; she might chop his head off.

Sitting, dangling his legs in the cold stream, he knew Princesses had such power. And who would speak up for him?

Not that there was much to live for. Family in the power of the Prince, land conquered, his love beyond him. And maybe so far beyond that he would not get to even see her. In this garb, he was a peasant – and peasants don't speak to princesses. But if he could get into the castle... He knew where her rooms were. And surely she would talk to him.

Surely?

He so wanted to see her again. Even though it would be the last time. Worlds away from the first.

While dwelling on the sad happiness of that hour, he heard the sound of a horse. He turned; a hay cart was lumbering towards him, drawn by a heavy white horse plodding methodically as if he could keep up that pace around the world. Cadd moved to give it room to go by, but the carter stopped it in the middle of the stream. And got down himself to drink, while his horse sank its grateful head into the water.

The carter wore a brown smock to just below his knees, and had a soft hat of the same colour with a mountain peak. He sipped out of cupped hands and wiped water over his brow and cheeks.

'Are you heading towards the castle?' said Cadd.

'I am,' said the carter, getting to his feet. 'In fact, going to that very place.'

'Might I have a lift?'

The carter grinned. 'If you can unload hay, boy?'

'I can.'

'Then I can give you a lift.'

Cadd gathered his things. He had his boots off, and the carter noted.

'How d'you lose the foot?'

'Soldiers,' he said.

'General Hal's army?'

'Yes,' said Cadd. Hal would do. Dead and gone, and an enemy hereabouts.

'Sound pair of boots, you have.'

'My uncle's a cobbler,' he said. 'He made a pair for a lord once. And said he'd do the same for me.'

'Good for him,' said the carter. 'Let's be on our way.'

He told Cadd to get on board. And while he did so, the carter led the reluctant horse out of the stream. Once away from the stream, the carter climbed up himself and whipped the horse onwards.

Cadd was pleased to ride, but not so pleased at the questions the carter put to him. And there was no escape. There, the two of them sat side by side, he and the curious carter. Cadd grew uncomfortable with all the answers he had given. Was he twisting himself in knots?

After about an hour or so the carter stopped the wagon at an inn.

'Look after the hay, boy.'

And went inside. Cadd was happy to do so, it wasn't an arduous job – and it was a rest from the questions. It seemed he was forever telling stories about who he was. Yesterday he was a Prince, today a peasant who had his foot cut off by General Hal's army and was visiting relatives, here and there. And had had to make up names and places, while the carter shrugged and said, 'Never heard of that one', which was no surprise as they were villages in Cadd's own country – and the people his relatives, who may or may not be still alive.

The carter was an age in the inn. Cadd wasn't unduly worried, as the man had said he had to be at the castle by evening. And however the horse plodded, or how many inns they stopped at – it would be easier than walking.

When the carter came out, perhaps two hours later, he was staggering. He gripped the wagon's side to keep himself from falling.

He said, 'Can you drive a wagon, boy?'

'Think so?'

'Does that mean yes or no?'

Cadd guessed what the man was going to ask, and said, 'Yes, I can.'

'Good,' said the carter. 'You drive. I'm going to have a sleep in the back.'

And with that he poked himself a hole in the hay and scrambled in.

Cadd had been told this was the castle road. And he knew something of horses now. He'd watched the wagoners when first on his way to Witland, and had watched this carter too. It seemed there was only two instructions that really mattered: stop and go.

He took up the whip and cracked it over the horse's head. The animal started off. And that mostly was that. There really wasn't a lot else for Cadd to do, providing the road didn't get busy. And he was free from the carter's questions. In the back, he could hear him snoring. Let him sleep all the way, thought Cadd; both would be happier.

Chapter 37

Later, it began to rain. Cadd pulled up his hood and hoped it would be a short storm, for the sake of himself, the horse and the hay. He didn't want to wake the man, as he'd hated the incessant questions – but wasn't sure what to do if it poured down. And it did, quickly drenching him and causing the horse, every so often, to shake itself in a flurry of spray.

Cadd halted the cart.

What was he to do? There was no shelter. And surely the hay must be covered. He didn't want to wake the carter, but might have to. He dropped to the ground and went to the back of the wagon. There he found a large rolled sheet with ropes attached. It must be a cover for the hay. Could he manage it himself?

He'd have a go.

The hay was a large mound in the wagon, about a man's height in the middle. Somewhere in it, the carter lay sleeping. Cadd could have found him by his snores, if he'd wished to – but he didn't. With great effort he unrolled the cloth over the heap, and realised it was too long. He had the length across the width. So arduously he twisted it round, having to balance on the wagon at various points to turn it. When he eventually managed it, he tied the cloth down at the four corners, hoping he'd done it right. He stepped back to look at his efforts. Though the cloth covered front and back, the sides were not well covered – but that was because the cloth wasn't wide enough. Though if he pulled it down tighter, compressing the hay, then it would cover better. So he went round once more, untying each rope and pulling them in tighter. And then the cloth was lopsided, so he did the rounds once more – wishing he'd woken the carter, as he was weary with his efforts and drenched to the skin.

It was only when he at last got back to the board that he found the carter's cape. Hardly worth putting it on, but he did so – and wished he had something for the horse, who was looking very downcast. But there was little he could do but continue.

Further up the road, he sheltered under a wide oak tree and watched the rain splatter into the puddles. The horse was half in and half out, but Cadd thought: hay first. He'd learnt that much from his father. Wet flour went mouldy and it must be the same with hay.

The rain slowed and he set the horse, once again, on his way. And in a little while, as the rain eased up, a rainbow arched across the sky, the hues so deep that they seemed just for him. The red, the yellow, the green, the purple; a sign that he was going the right way, that he was doing what he must. Slowly the colours faded, and the clouds cleared from the sky. The horse steamed as it plodded in the welcoming sunlight.

And, after the rainbow, another welcome. For there at last was the castle, its white towers shining and banners flying. He would be there in an hour or two.

Chapter 38

A few hundred yards from the castle, he woke the carter, who cursed and grumbled at being disturbed, and then complained about the way the cloth was tied over the hay.

'I'm not going into the castle with it tied up like that. I'm not.'

As they untied the ropes, Cadd thought it was like being back with his father. You did your best, and he still moaned at you. But he knew he must not talk back, and apologised for doing it so badly, which the carter grudgingly accepted. They rolled the cloth and stowed it in the back. And the carter went around feeling the hay.

'Not so bad,' he said. 'Could've been worse.'

Cadd needed to stay on the good side of the carter to get into the castle. And was grateful for the hood the peasant had given him, for the castle knew the Prince – and he did not wish to be known. Simply to be taken as the carter's man. That is, until he got to the Princess.

They were stopped at the drawbridge by the guard.

'For the stables,' said the carter.

'I see you've got a new hand,' said the soldier, causing Cadd to look down at his boots in case he might be recognised.

The guard waved them in.

The cart rumbled over the drawbridge and into the courtyard. There the carter climbed down and led the horse towards the stables. Cadd looked about the courtyard; he could see the entrance he had to get to, where the Princess' chambers were. There was a guard at the entrance, somehow he'd have to get past him. And, he knew, another at the top of the stairs… His neck prickled. This was dangerous work. The guards were to stop peasants getting to the Princess – and yet he must evade them.

He had no clear plan.

It would be easier in the dark, he hoped. He would help the carter unload, and then disappear. Hide somewhere until nightfall. The soldiery made him shiver. He counted six at various points and knew there were others.

There was another option; he could leave with the carter. Abandon the Princess to the Prince. But if he did that, then nothing had meaning. He would despise his own cowardice. But he would at least be alive.

The cart stopped by the stables. There was a stench of manure; inside he could see a straw-scattered floor and horses tethered in stalls. He'd been inside as the Prince, and knew there were many more he couldn't see. Here were the royal horses and the horses for the King's cavalry.

The stablemaster came out, a stocky man in a leather apron. He examined the hay and complained about the dampness. The carter blamed his hand and cuffed Cadd round the ear. Another time, he might have told the carter to get a bigger sheet – but thought it best to take the blame. As a carter's man would.

It was decided to use the damp outer layer for current feed – and store the rest. Cadd did what he was told. He took a pitchfork and unloaded this portion there, and that over there.

The carter moaned at him. 'Have you never used a pitchfork before?'

Cadd hadn't but didn't say so. The work was hard as he hadn't fully recovered, and neither did he have the knack. He told himself – he must do his best, this won't last long. Accept the moans and the cuffs. He'd have earned his ride when he finished this job – and that would be the last he'd ever see of the carter. Good riddance.

By the time the wagon was empty, it was growing dark. The carter went to get his payment from the stablemaster, and Cadd eased away into the shadows of the stable. He covered himself with hay and thought to hide for an hour or so. By then it would be night and there was more chance he could get around the castle unseen.

In his heap he heard the carter calling, but he had had more than enough of the carter. It was a temporary employment only. He lay quietly in the hay. The calling ceased; evidently the man had realised he no longer had a hand. And a little later he heard the wagon leaving.

He might have left with the carter, but had lost that choice. Now, leaving would be as hard as staying. Either way there were soldiers with spears to pass. He thought of those very first soldiers, the ones who had taken him away from his family. His eyes welled. Almost anything could conjure up thoughts of his mother, his father and brothers. Some little thing and he was a boy helping his mother make cakes. He wiped his eyes with his sleeve. He had come a long from the bakery. And he wondered how much further he was to go.

When Cadd judged it dark enough, he crept out of the stable and into the courtyard. His hood was fully over his head as he edged round the wall. A few lanterns were lit in the yard, and shadowy people hurried about their business. Cadd kept to the areas of darkness as he made his way round the courtyard.

He stopped by a buttress perhaps five yards from the Princess' entrance. Cadd could just make out the guard from the light of the lantern hanging above his head. He was at one side of the door, holding an upright spear, halting the unauthorised. How was he to get past him? The guard had a post; he did not patrol. There was no way by him but in his sight.

Very well. This would work or it wouldn't. He drew off his hood.

And strode to the guard.

'I am the Prince of Larken,' he said. 'I have come to see the Princess.'

The guard said, 'I haven't heard anyone was coming...'

'Do you doubt me, soldier?'

'No one told me...' he said weakly.

Cadd came up close, under the lantern.

'Do you know me?'

'Yes, Your Highness. I'm sorry... Please enter.'

'I shall refer you to your captain,' said Cadd as he walked confidently past into the hallway.

Then up the stone steps, his heart beating like festival bells. One guard past. He sighed with relief and did not look back. The guard had recognised him as the Prince. The bad light had worked for him. And his peasant's garb hadn't betrayed him.

At the top of the steps he stopped. Ahead was the corridor leading to the Princess' chambers. There were a few lanterns on the wall along its length. And there, outside her room, was the second guard he must get by.

There was no other way; he must play the Prince. He wished he had his former clothes, and cursed that they had been buried. But it was foolish to mourn for them. He was here as he was. His only chance was to be Prince Grude.

He hesitated, mouth dry, breathing rapidly. He must calm down – or create suspicion. Authority was the only way through. He clenched his fists, digging his nails into his palms and attempted breathing regularly.

And then a thought; it was lighter here, he needed authority. A Prince would come with servants; he had no servants. Then he would get one at least. He withdrew and took a few steps down the stairway.

He called, 'Guard!'

'Yes, Your Highness,' replied the soldier at the entrance.

'Come up here.'

The guard came. A measured step, along the hallway, up the steps. As he came towards him, Cadd could see how young he was. Hardly older than he himself. All to his advantage.

'I should not leave my post, Your Highness,' said the guard nervously.

'I will put it right with your officers. Come with me.'

And Cadd walked slowly and confidently down the hallway, with the guard following. He had his authority. The guard ahead was watching his approach. Cadd did not speed up, but walked as if these were his corridors. As if he had a right to be here, followed by his guard.

He stopped before the guard at the Princess' door. He allowed the guard behind to catch up before speaking, as if the guard were part of him – and it might be said he was.

'I am the Prince of Larken,' said Cadd. 'I have come to see the Princess.'

The guard bowed nervously, glancing at the guard behind.

'Your Highness,' he said. 'I'm sorry, I cannot let you in.'

'Whyever not?' barked Cadd.

'I have no authority, Your Highness. I must stop everyone. No one comes without an equerry.'

'I don't know Witland customs,' said Cadd, working to keep the authority in his voice. This guard was older. He had firmer orders. How could Cadd persuade him? Having got so close…

'I cannot let you in, Your Highness.' His eyes were twitching and he was trembling. 'Orders. I cannot help it, Your Highness. I am not allowed to.'

'I demand you let me in. Or I shall report you to your captain.'

The guard looked about him desperately. 'Can you not send the guard for an equerry?'

Cadd knew he could not. Nor could he leave. He was a Prince. There was no way but on. And if he was not allowed forward...

Without warning, he banged on the door with his fist.

He yelled, 'The Prince of Larken is here!'

The guard stood aside in shock. And so did Cadd. He had done it now. Broken protocol. He waited for the reaction, pressing against the door, trying to hold his body still. The silence was shattering; both guards watched the door as if frozen. The forbidden had been done. Cadd's teeth would not stop chattering. But he must hold fast. This was the time. He would see her and he would tell her. He would get through. He would explain. Or his journey was in vain.

The door slowly opened.

Cadd faced front and tried to breathe easily. His legs were hollow, his stomach beating like a drum.

And there, between the opening double doors, stood Bild, holding a lantern, his face twisted in puzzled anger.

'What are you doing here, Your Highness?' He turned to the soldiers. 'Stand away, guards.'

The guards stepped out of earshot with relief. This was no longer their business.

Bild lifted his lantern up and down, staring at Cadd's clothing. 'I don't understand, Your Highness. You are on the way to Larken... Why are you dressed this way?'

Cadd sucked his lips; he had difficulty speaking. He pressed his hands to his thighs to stop them shaking.

'I am not the Prince, Bild,' he at last said.

'Loo was not lying then,' said Bild, taking half a step back and holding the lantern as high as he could, and peering into Cadd's face. 'I wondered about you.'

'I came here as the Prince. But I am not the Prince. And it's why I must speak to Princess Rosalie. I must explain the reasons.'

Bild shook his head. 'I always knew there was something about you. Something unprincely.' He half smiled. 'It was to your credit.'

'Can I speak to the Princess?' he whispered.

Bild rubbed his cheek. 'I'll see what I can do.'

He retreated, closing the door behind him. Cadd breathed easier. At last she would know he was here. And, surely, would want to know what had happened. Why he had done what he had done. The two guards were about five yards to either side of him, standing to attention, their spears by their sides. They believed they were in the presence of a prince, reflected Cadd, outside the chambers of a princess. No place for sloppiness.

This might take some time. Bild explaining the little he knew, Bild persuading... He strode backwards and forwards between the guards, as if they were the outposts of his territory. And wondered how the Princess was taking what Bild had to say. It would be shocking news. Bild though was on his side. He would put him in the best light – surely?

But what was the best light? Bild had little to go on. Cadd had simply told him he wasn't the Prince. No explanation – and so Bild could give none. He had impetuously said he wasn't the Prince, which Bild half knew anyway. Should he have claimed he really was the Prince? But Bild would have been suspicious. And these clothes... How stupid! He should have worn the peasant's garb for the journey – but kept the Prince's clothes for the castle.

It didn't matter what he might have done; the Prince's clothes were buried. And Cadd had told Bild he wasn't the Prince – and that was that. He was where he was, wearing what he had on. So... He leaned against the wall and tried to still his nerves. How would she greet him? How he should he greet her? It was no longer Princess to Prince but Princess to commoner. He was so beneath her, would he even be allowed to speak?

Why was Bild so long? This was tortuous. What was he saying? How was she reacting? At least Cadd hoped he could clear things up. Tell her the truth. Save her. Save himself. And then go his way, wherever that might be. This must end.

The door opened.

Bild was there again.

'What did she say?' he said, searching the dwarf's face for warning.

Bild clapped his hands. 'Guards.' They looked to him. 'Take him to the dungeon.'

Chapter 39

The straw stank of urine, but he had no choice but to sit in it. There were things crawling within but he could not see what they were. Perhaps as well. While the door had been open, he had seen a small high window, but it let in no light now it was night.

He'd hoped at least she would have spoken to him. Given him the chance to explain. But it seems swans don't speak to swine.

He could have wept for his stupidity.

He'd got close. Done well – all considered. Got to her door, had it opened, got a message to her... What more could be asked?

To speak to her. That was what he had wanted – simply to speak to her. But she was at the top of the mountain and he down in the deepest chasm. He could scream and yell and break his bones on these walls – and she would not know.

Or care.

He'd damned himself. Thrown himself in the grave. What a fool's errand! Escaping from Loo's sack did not mean he had a charmed life. Rather that he had run out of lives. Pushed his luck this once too often.

Now what?

He could stay here forever. Or for however long you survived in a dungeon. Much less than forever. The room stank of its past residents. Of their despair and bodily functions. How long can you stare at a wall? He hadn't had any food, but knew it would be awful. The leavings of the leavings.

This straw would be his shroud.

He might be executed. That would be no surprise. He had taken on the identity of a prince. That was a treason of treasons. And he had no defenders. He was a stranger too. So why give him dungeon room? Or spare a mouldy crust?

Or they might torture him. And thinking about it, that was most likely. Find out exactly what had gone on. Get a confession, signed in his blood. Well, he'd say the worst of the Prince. Damn him to hell. And then he might get what he wanted: the Princess renouncing her betrothal. Not that Cadd's plans had involved torture and execution, though he suspected the latter might be a blessing when it came.

He had come a long way.

He remembered the rainbow he had seen earlier that day, the peasant family that had helped him – and got him thinking that the world was not simply wicked. Was that a trick of fate – to make him want to rescue his beloved?

A dungeon was not a fair reward for honesty. But whoever said the world was fair? What fool? Fair to his brothers, fair to his parents? Fair to him? No. Bakers' sons hoped for luck, not for fairness. That they would not be crushed under the feet of princesses.

She would not see him.

He should have anticipated that. He'd had an education in the ways of royalty. He'd met kings. Two. Been a prince of sorts. Kissed a princess even. It would be good to go on. To feel he was loved… And he had thought he was, for an hour or so. A sad dream. It was the Prince that was loved. Not the son of a baker.

She'd thrown him in the dungeon…

His mind circled in its darkness. There was no sleep. He had come as far as he could. Was she sleeping? It had been a lovely hour with her. The only girl he had ever kissed. But it had been a lie anyway – and for that he must die. There would be no mourners, no hymns sung. He would have liked longer – but does anyone get to choose? The axe comes down when the axeman chooses.

Cadd wept.

For his short life, for his family, for a love that would never be. Because he was alone and frightened. Because of the dark, the cold, the stench. Because there would be no mercy.

A key turned in the lock.

Was it food or torture?

Chapter 40

The door swung wide. Bild was in the entrance holding a lantern. He stepped into the cell. Behind him was a figure, a little taller, in a long robe and cowl, who followed the dwarf inside. Bild swung his lantern round the cell and grimaced at the smell.

Cadd rose to greet them.

The other figure swept off the cowl. It was the Princess. Her hair fell to her waist, the lantern reflected in her dark eyes.

Cadd bowed. 'Your Highness.'

'You wish to speak to me,' she said. Her voice was cold, ungiving.

'I am unworthy…' He sank to his knees before her.

'Yes, you are,' she said. 'Now stand up.'

Cadd rose. She crossed to him and slapped him round the face. The blow rocked him.

'How dare you treat me this way!' Her body was shaking with anger. 'I have never been so humiliated.' She paced around the cell, wringing her hands, her hunchback quivering under her dark robe. 'I told my father I was betrothed. I told my relatives. Messengers have been sent throughout the land. Everyone awaits the return of the Prince…' She turned to him blazing. 'And he comes back – as a vagabond.'

Cadd was once more on his knees before her storm.

'I have no words to express my sorrow, Your Highness.'

She grasped his hair and pulled his head back. 'You are a nobody. A liar.'

Cadd had no reply.

'And I'm a fool to be here.'

She let go of his head. It sank forward in penitence.

'You gave me happiness,' she said wearily. 'I thought here was the Prince I could marry. Here was the man I could love and who would love me.' She sank to his level and said quietly, 'Instead I have a jumped-up peasant, a jester who juggled with me instead of with coloured balls.' She shook her head. 'I don't know who you are. I don't know why you have done it. And I am the saddest girl on earth.'

She stood up and stepped away from him.

'And I don't know why you have come back.'

Cadd lifted his head. There were tears on her cheeks.

'I came to tell you, Your Highness, that you must not marry the Prince.'

She threw her head back and gave a half laugh. 'Marry you? Now!'

'No,' said Cadd. 'The Prince.'

She stepped up to him. 'What are you talking about?'

'He is coming to claim you.'

She looked to Bild, who shrugged in incomprehension.

'Who is coming?' she exclaimed. 'Make yourself clear.'

'Prince Grude is coming. He will be here in a few days. He is coming to claim you.'

'You keep saying that,' she shouted into his face. 'How can he come to claim me? It was to you I made my promise.'

Cadd bowed his head. 'I am his shadow, Your Highness. He sent me in his place.'

She threw her hands wide and kicked the straw.

'At last it becomes plain,' she declared. 'You came to woo me in his stead. You – a copy, a likeness. And he claims the prize.'

Cadd could not speak. It was out. She knew.

'Was this a game? Something dreamed up in cards and in drink... Play a hand for the Princess.'

'Your Highness, I did not come to Witland to deceive you...'

'But you did.'

He nodded. 'I did, Your Highness. But I came to save my family...'

'What have your family to do with wooing me?'

'I had to woo you – or they would die.' He bowed his head. 'But they are dead now, I fear. Or very soon will be. And I am here to tell you, it is all a lie. I am not the Prince. He did not woo you. And you must not marry him. He is a beast.'

'More beastly than you?'

'Much more.'

She turned to the dwarf, her hands turned up.

'What do you make of this, Bild?'

'Your Highness, I think we have a story to hear. I don't think he is wicked. Why return if he were?'

She turned back to Cadd, who was on his knees.

'He is your protector, whoever you are. Bild speaks for you. And I wonder why. What he sees in you.' She paced about the cell, kicking straw. 'Or perhaps I do know. I saw it when we met.' She came back to him. 'Were you wooing me for the Prince?'

'I was and I wasn't, Your Highness. When I was with you, I forgot about him. I fell in love with you.'

'To save your family?'

'No.' He raised his head. 'I, with you. No family, no Prince. I, with you.'

She lifted his chin. 'But who are you?' She turned to Bild. 'Get me a stool. There's more to hear.'

Bild put down the lantern.

'Yes, Your Highness.'

He began to leave but she stopped him.

'Get three. We may be some time.'

Chapter 41

When they were alone, she said, 'I fell in love with you, you know.'

'And I was the happiest man alive when I left you.'

She walked about kicking at the straw. 'This cell is horrible. I am sorry I put you here.'

'I am sorry I deceived you.'

'I thought of chopping your head off. Torturing you...' She stopped. 'You hurt me so much.'

'I came to save you.'

She laughed. 'Do you know what hurt me most? I'm sure you don't. It was your commoner's hands. They had touched me. They had massaged me – and made me love you.' She snorted. 'I thought of chopping them off too. You see what rank does to you? You see how proud I am?' She shook her head, her hair flying out. 'You made me so happy. You make me so unhappy. I could draw and quarter you.'

'Do what you want to me – but don't marry the Prince.'

She chuckled mirthlessly. 'I don't think you need fear that. And I shan't draw and quarter you. Though you deserve it. I shall free you – for the hour of happiness you gave me.'

'And now we are both unhappy,' he said.

'Yes.' She gave a weary sigh. 'And the trouble you have given me. I shall have to tell everyone that I am withdrawing my promise. How on earth shall I explain that without seeming a fool? What shall I say to my father? My relatives? What will we tell the people?' She turned to him. 'It might be easier marrying a beast.'

'No. It won't.'

'I'd rather marry you,' she said. 'But that's impossible. With your commoner's hands still attached to your

commoner's body. So I shall return to my spinsterhood…
Sadder but wiser.'

Bild returned, holding a three-legged stool. Behind him
followed a gaoler, carrying two more. He put them down
and Bild dismissed him. The gaoler clumsily bowed and
left.

They placed the three stools in a tight triangle and took
one each.

'Now, my false Prince,' she said. 'Tell me how you
became such a liar.'

And Cadd began.

He told her about his family, his father the baker, his
mother, his brothers. And how one day, during the siege,
the soldiers came for the fourth son of the fourth son of a
baker. He told her how he was taken to the King and his
witch. How she gave him the gift, and the message he was
told to give to General Hal to save the town. He told her
how he came down the walls and crossed the lines. How he
crossed the river and found the witch's gift worked. And
how, on the other side, trying to get round the enemy lines
– he was caught in a mantrap, and woke in the General's
tent with one foot.

He told her how he would have been executed if the
Prince had not come and they had not seen that Cadd was
the Prince's double, down even to the detail of a missing
foot. He told her about his education, learning about the
Prince, eating like the Prince while chained up in a tent.
And how at last the Prince had decided that his double
must woo the Princess for him, while the Prince won the
glory when Tolga fell. And the promise: that Cadd's family
would be saved if he wooed her successfully. He told her
how in the three days' journey to Witland he had to learn to
walk in his new boots, how Loo the insufferable taught him

to ride until Loo was banished to his tent. And how Loo escaped.

She knew much of his time in Witland. His arrival, the banquet, the three tasks and of course his audience with her – so he shortened this, adding more only when she questioned him. He told her how he'd been captured by Loo when he returned to his room. Tied up, thrust in a sack into a chest, and carried away. His sudden disappearance explained by his father's illness – but the promised return. He told her of his escape from the river, his decision to come to the castle. And finally, his journey here.

When he had finished, the Princess was quiet.

The three were in their huddle on the stools, knees almost touching. Their faces flickering and shadowy in the lamplight.

At last she said, 'I knew you were remarkable.'

'I simply wanted to stay alive,' he said.

'Do you still want to marry me?'

'I can't.'

'That's not what I asked you,' she said sharply.

He hesitated. She touched his hand. He could just see her eyes seeking his in the dim light.

'I do,' he said.

She squeezed his hand. 'Then you shall.'

'But how?'

'You must be the Prince once more, come to claim his bride.'

'But how can I? I have no horses, no retinue.'

She flapped a hand dismissively. 'I can give you all that.'

'The Prince's clothes are still here in his rooms,' added Bild.

'So there you are,' she said brightly. 'All you need.'

'But the Prince himself is coming here in three days…' exclaimed Cadd.

She laughed and clapped her hands. 'And what will he walk into? A Prince already here.'

'But I shall be exposed.'

'You will not, my love.'

'Why not?'

'Because I shall stand by you. And there can be but one Prince. And that must be you.' She put a finger to his lips to stop any protest. 'I insist. And you are not yet the Prince. So I shall be obeyed. Do you hear?'

'I hear.'

She laughed. 'I am so glad I didn't chop your hands off.'

Chapter 42

An hour or so later, Cadd and Bild rode out of the castle. It was still dark, though the first streaks of dawn were appearing on the horizon. Bild was a good rider, it was part of his bag of tricks; he could do handstands on a galloping horse. But Cadd could neither do handstands or feel comfortable at a gallop, and so Bild moderated his pace to fit.

Once away from the castle, they slowed to rest the horses.

'It's good to be in the open air,' said Cadd. 'To be away from the castle.'

'It's important to get you away while it's dark,' said the dwarf. 'The fewer that see you the better.'

'Not many would see me in the dungeon.'

'I'll take you back if you wish.'

'No thank you.'

The end of the night was chilly with low-lying mist. Both of them rode with their hoods up.

'Would she really have executed me?' enquired Cadd.

Bild laughed. 'She has a temper. When I told her you weren't in fact the Prince... Well, let's say – you were better off in the dungeon.'

'I can't believe all that's happened in the last few hours.'

'Quite a turnabout,' said Bild. 'Mind you, it's her father I'd worry about if I were you. He's the one going to need convincing when it comes to saying who's the real Prince.'

'He's got a temper too.'

'Runs in the family,' said Bild.

'Oh, but isn't she amazing...'

'And she might yet get your head chopped off. Think about it. She could have sent you on your way easily enough.'

'But then I wouldn't be able to marry her.'

'Or risk losing your head.' Bild shrugged. 'Your choice. You could ride off now. Be away.'

Cadd was thoughtful. 'Would she have me brought back?'

'I doubt it,' said Bild. 'She'd know why you'd gone.'

'Then I'll take my chances.'

'At what?'

'At marrying a princess.'

Bild snorted. 'You deserve each other.'

They rode for about two hours. It was light but still chilly when they halted at a copse of thin trees.

'Stay out of sight,' said Bild. 'I'll return with your retinue at noon.'

'Thank you, Bild.'

'Don't thank me. I want Princess Rosalie to marry someone who will appreciate her.'

'I do.'

'And if you are lying – then I'll chop your head off.'

Bild rode off, leaving him. Cadd led his horse into the copse. He tied it up. And sat back against a tree trunk. He had food and water with him. Bild had grabbed it from the kitchen in their hurried exit. Once the plan had come out, then the enactment began almost at once. Time mattered if he was to steal a few days on the Prince. And establish himself.

He thought of Bild's words. Yes, he could ride off. Go wherever. Start a new life. And he knew she wasn't likely to drag him back. What for? With the Prince coming in a few days – why complicate her life with a reluctant impostor? But he wasn't going to ride away. So there'd be no test for her. He had a chance and he would take it. But he knew too it wasn't the walk in the woods that Rosalie made it sound. Prince Grude would fight like a bear for his identity.

It would be a fight to the death. For the loser would be unlikely to survive.

But she loved him. And, strange world – could only be his if he were a prince. In stories woodcutters married princesses, but that was the silliness of stories, as his mother would say. He wondered why they were told, when it couldn't happen. Woodcutters married peasant girls, milkmaids or woodcutters' daughters. They never met princesses – who would despise them anyway. Or imagine the King's reaction if he, a baker's son, turned up and asked for the hand of his daughter?

Cadd laughed. He'd ask how many castles his father had.

But she loved him. Always left him soppy this way. In disbelief that anyone could love him. He who had made such a mess of things, and lost a foot in the process. And that surely was worth fighting for?

It was, of course, why he'd returned to the castle. Yes, to warn her, but really to see her once more. And to hope against hope that a woodcutter could very occasionally marry a princess.

Chapter 43

Bild returned a little after noon with a wagon. It had been filled with several of the Prince's chests, left behind in the castle. The retinue were waiting a few miles up the road. It was time for Cadd to become the Prince.

He washed in a stream, wiping away the stink of the dungeon. And dressed in the princely clothes that Bild had brought. A silk shirt, a green jacket with gold embroidery, a hat to match. His leggings were blue – only the boots were kept, especially made for him, and these Bild cleaned and shined.

Bild sat him on a stool and gave him a shave. He trimmed Cadd's hair.

'I feel something like a prince,' he said.

'You are the Prince,' said Bild. And bowed. 'Your Highness.'

'I could still ride away – you know,' mused Cadd.

'You could,' agreed Bild. 'But I wouldn't in those clothes.'

Cadd laughed. 'How can I take this beautiful jacket off?' He stroked the sleeves. 'Though I might wish I had.'

They buried the peasant garb. The irony was not lost on Cadd. Somewhere, buried – was a prince's garb. He was not used to this disposal of clothing. They were handed down in his family, or given away if there was any wear left in them. The waste in burying good clothes was hurtful.

But necessary.

There must be no signs of a changeover. He would ride in as if he had come from Larken. Returned after four days away. His father, it had turned out, was not very ill – and had recovered by the time he had arrived. And so the Prince was free to return to his betrothed.

They left the copse. Both on the wagon board, with Cadd's horse tied to the rear. They discussed the detail: the things they had planned and the things they could not. The Prince, the real one, was expected in two to three days. In that time Cadd must establish himself.

He would have time and surprise on his side. For Prince Grude believed Cadd was dead. Drowned in a sack weighed down with stones.

When the retinue were in sight, Cadd mounted his own horse – and rode ahead of the wagon. The soldiers of the retinue bowed as he rode in, and he acknowledged them with a nod. He spoke only to the captain, and asked him to ride behind with the troop. The Prince would take the lead to the castle.

None of the soldiers had any insignia of Witland. They must not be seen as Rosalie's guard. And once at the castle, they would melt away. It was a difficulty they had acknowledged – but some story could be made of their absence. Hunting, out on an exercise – and when the Prince's troop rode in, in two days, then Cadd could claim them.

He hoped, in all the pomp, the identity of his retinue would not be noticed. After all, no one would suspect he was not the true prince.

Not until the other arrived.

After several miles, two of the retinue galloped ahead to warn the castle of his imminent arrival. So then it would begin again. The bowing, the exaggerated compliments, the stream of lies he must tell about his country, his father the King, and why he had come back so swiftly.

The thought of it exhausted him. But it must be gone through. And he had done it before, so was at least forewarned. He had the Princess and Bild on his side this time. But only two days, perhaps three, to be so utterly the

Prince – that the arrival of another would be greeted with disbelief.

At least he could ride. And now there would be no archery contest. No Princess to win. Simply her father; he was the one who must be won. He would determine truth or falsity.

The castle was in sight. As they rode closer, the crowds came out and lined the road on both sides, not only from the castle itself but swelled by those from local villages. On this occasion, he was not a visitor but the betrothed of their Princess.

He straightened his back in regal stance. This would ache by the time he came to the gates – but majesty was expected and he must play to it. As he reached the edge of the crowd he raised a hand in greeting, but looked neither to the right or left. He was the proud Prince returning.

After a little way, his hand ached. Carefully, he took it down and half a minute or so later raised the other. His back was stiff, he wanted to shrug his shoulders, scratch – but such human things he was not at liberty to do. This last half mile would be a long one.

From the gates of the castle he heard a commotion. The King, he thought, is coming to meet me. He went through the exchanges as the figure on horseback came towards him: ruler of this and that, beloved by God and his angels, honoured by, courageous in battle, esteemed, his exploits told in saga and song...

Except it wasn't the King.

Riding towards him was Princess Rosalie on a black horse. She wore a red dress, with a flowing white silken headdress – and on it a small crown that caught the sunlight. Her long tresses hung over her shoulders. He could not see her hunchback from this forward position, but knew the stress of her riding so exposed, so public. She was doing this for him. Coming to greet her betrothed, the Prince. Behind her danced handmaidens in light green dresses, each with twirling ribbons of red and yellow in either hand.

Rosalie was smiling at his surprise. And Cadd was smiling too, at what she was prepared to do. This greeting they had not spoken about, Bild had not warned him. So much better than all the formality with her father. That, of course, would come.

But not yet.

When he was perhaps fifty yards away, she stopped and turned her horse about. The handmaidens came past her, their ribbons skipping, and once past her, turned around. They were waiting for him.

He came slowly forward, the cheering going on and on. And then he reached her; the handmaidens curtseyed and gave him room. He did not stop, knowing she was a better rider than he was – and could well fit with him.

In a few strides she was by his side. He did not look at her, but could feel her and catch the impression of her silks out of the corner of his eye. He wanted to touch her, to say something – but it was too public for intimacy. Easily, she fixed his pace, and they rode in side by side, the handmaidens dancing behind.

And then came a swelling of trumpets. This time, he knew, it must be the King. And out from the castle he came, on a black stallion. He wore a long cloak made of the fur of a white bear, on his head a weighty crown, and in his right hand a jewelled sceptre. He was not to be outshone by his daughter. Slowly King and betrothed pair converged, to the sound of the trumpets and the cheering of the crowd.

Cadd felt a touch. It was her hand. He took it and their fingers entwined. And he was filled with both happiness and fear. Fear that they would know him, see he wasn't who he claimed. But happiness won; he knew she would protect him. He was her Prince.

At least for now.

Before the King reached them, he stopped his horse and turned about. And waited for them. When they were about ten yards away, he set his horse walking – and led them through the cheering throng to his castle.

It was a welcome without words, which Cadd was grateful for. But he saw the significance of it, and knew why Rosalie had set this up. So that her father and everyone would see him as her Prince. She and he, side by side. She and he, holding hands as they rode into the castle. That was the image Prince Grude would have to smash when he came to claim his prize.

Once in the castle courtyard, there were few about. It was ghostly; the castle had been abandoned by even its kitchen maids and boot boys. A solitary groom waited. They dismounted, he took their horses, and the King led the way to his own chambers.

Chapter 44

In the chambers another surprise awaited, and one less to his liking. They had gone in to a tower, climbing stone stairs to a circular room. Two servants who had stayed behind stood either side of a heaving table, ready to serve. But seated on a sofa, and rising to greet them, was the King's mistress.

He had forgotten her name, having only seen her once at the King's banquet – and there barely, as she was mostly hidden by a prince and the King. He was surprised by her youth; she wasn't much older than Rosalie. She wore a long, deep blue dress to her ankles with puffed shoulders. On her head was a heart shaped bonnet with her golden hair streaming out at the front and sides. She had a dusting of freckles on her face and was lightly painted. Cadd found her overwhelming; she was the most beautiful woman he had ever seen.

But knew, too, this was wrong.

One glance at Rosalie's face convinced him of it. Her face was dark with anger. All lightness had gone; she was encompassed in storm clouds, ready to break imminently.

The lady was holding out her hand. Cadd was thrown. This was a greeting he must make, and, however he did it, must offend someone.

He bowed low, took the hand, and kissed it.

He said, 'Long have I heard of your beauty, madam – and they lie. For it is twice as much.'

And nearly died of shame. Not that she wasn't beautiful – that was sincere enough – but the hurt he knew he was inflicting on Rosalie. Yet he couldn't damn himself before the King. For it was he who would decide Cadd's future.

This was another test. Worse than the archery. He did not know Rosalie well enough. Could he be losing her now, as he gained the favour of the King and his mistress? He did not dare look at her.

'Princess Rosalie has picked the best of the three,' said the lady as he came out of his bow. She took his hand. 'Come sit by me. I wish to know you better.'

Cadd had no choice but to accompany her. He knew this was a taunt. She was deliberately taking him away from the Princess, as if she were the Queen herself. As if this ceremony were totally for him to meet her. And perhaps it was. She had, after all, been waiting as the King brought them in.

This family would take some fitting in to.

He sat next to her. He knew by the extravagant attention paid to him that a game was being played. Within it he was a toy, the game was not really for him – but for Rosalie and the King.

The King's mistress complimented him; she asked him questions and embarrassed him intensely with her blue staring eyes. She was flirting with him, and really he was too easy, she who had conquered a king. Her beauty melted him and he did not feel much of a prince at all. He knew if she continued, he might lose the King too. And yet he could not leave her.

He was helpless. Never had he had such beauty flooded onto him. Never had he met anyone remotely like her – not any of the women and girls who came into his father's bakery. She was the sun, and he the sunflower who could not take his gaze off her.

Rosalie rescued him.

'Let me show you the view,' she said.

She dragged him up. And he knew that if the lady had resisted with a single small finger he would not have gone – but she let him go.

They crossed the room and looked out the window, but neither saw the view.

'I hate that woman,' hissed Rosalie.

Cadd nodded. It was obvious why. He was still shivering, after an encounter which meant little to the lady, but which had held him like a minnow in a net.

Rosalie turned to her father and his mistress, holding her betrothed firmly by the arm.

'We shall go up to the battlement, Father.'

'Show him the Kingdom, my dear,' the King nodded benignly.

They crossed to a small door. Rosalie opened it, revealing twisting stone steps, and all but pushed him out. She closed the door after them, and they climbed the stairs out into the open air of the tower battlement.

'She's a viper,' exclaimed Rosalie.

'She is beautiful,' he said feebly.

'Oh, you men are all the same,' she snorted. 'See how she has my father? And see how much more she wants? She knows she can get it. The fool dotes on her.' She poked Cadd in the chest. 'And see what she did to you? My betrothed! How dare she! How dare you!'

She turned away, the wind catching her hair.

Cadd came behind and put his hand on her shoulder. She threw his hand away.

'She doesn't want me,' said Cadd.

'Lucky you,' she said disdainfully. 'You'd be no trouble.'

Cadd didn't know how to get out of this. He was still trembling from his meeting. And knew she was right. He had no resistance to the lady.

He said, 'She is incredibly beautiful.'

'And she knows how to use it,' said Rosalie bitterly.

'What on earth is her name?' he said. 'I've forgotten. And I can't ask her.'

'Lady Lula,' said Rosalie. 'And anyone less of a lady I've yet to meet.'

'How do we get out of here?' he said.

'There's no way but through that room,' she said.

'Then let's stay here a little while,' he said. 'I need my strength to face them.' Rosalie still had her back to him. He held her shoulders; this time she did not resist. 'I am so sorry, but this is so difficult for me. I have to win people over. I barely know what I am doing.'

'You do really want to marry me?' she said.

'Why else should I come back?'

'For a kingdom?'

He shook his head. 'Keep it. I've never dreamed of kingdoms. But there was a girl who bathed me once... Who did not care I had lost my foot.'

'And there was a boy who loved a hunchback.'

'And still does.'

'You have conquered me,' she said. 'And now let's see if we can leave without offending.'

Chapter 45

They returned to the King and his mistress with the intention of leaving them as soon as they could. But this was not so easy. When the King said stay a while, it was impossible for Cadd not to obey. To do so would give offence. Rosalie on her own would have done, bad manners or not, but she had to stay for Cadd. And with the same protective motive, she took the opportunity to sit next to the lady. Cadd sat by the King, and was at once interrogated by him. How was his father, how had he managed to get back so quickly – questions to which he had worked out the answers with Bild on their ride to the copse. Bild, though, had suggested another strategy: get the King talking about hunting and his dogs. And, as soon as there was a pause, Cadd said, 'I hear you are a great hunter, Your Majesty,' and noted that Rosalie, who was not saying a word to the mistress but listening in, smiled.

The King talked on about his hunting. And on about his dogs. And made it harder for Rosalie to get Cadd away. At one point he was barely listening and glanced at the King's mistress, one of many stolen glances, but this one she met – and the look she gave in return hollowed him. He turned away, trembling, and listened to the finer points of hunting dogs.

At last Rosalie grew impatient. She bounced off her couch and took Cadd by the arm.

'We must see the rose garden before dark, Father.'

'I was telling him about my dogs, daughter. Man talk.'

'Tell him tomorrow. Come on.'

'If it pleases you, Your Majesty…' Cadd said awkwardly, pulled along by Rosalie.

'Go on, go on,' said the King, flapping him away. 'There will be a hunt tomorrow. You will see the dogs…'

Cadd bowed to the lady. 'It has been a great pleasure to meet you, Lady Lula.'

'Mine entirely,' she said.

And her smile chopped away his legs and would have had him saying farewell forever if Rosalie had not dragged him away.

In the courtyard, as they crossed to the rose garden, he said, 'I cannot resist her.'

'Neither can my father,' said Rosalie dryly. 'I have watched him the last two years. And Lula can do whatever she wishes with him. I hope not to witness the same with you.'

'I don't like her,' he said, 'But I simply can't resist her.'

'Luckily she is spoken for. Unless you want to lose your head.'

'I've enough opportunities for that,' he said, 'without adding another.'

They entered the King's rose garden. There was no one else there, as they wandered through the pergolas in the lengthening shadows. She showed him her favourites, the most colourful, the most scented. They sat under a bower and watched the sun set.

'I like it here, this time of year,' she said. 'The last roses still hanging on.'

'There is a banquet tonight,' he said. 'Will that be a trial?'

'I hope not,' she said. 'I told him – if it's simply another meat feast and drunken debauch then I'm not coming. He said I must, that you and I were the guests of honour. I said, then I had to help plan it. And so, there will be fewer guests, less wine, better wine than the rotgut he usually serves – and other dishes apart from meat, meat, meat. And there will be entertainment; but I said it must be heard too.'

A little later, they parted to prepare for the banquet in an hour. Cadd went to the chambers reserved for him, the same as before, where his effects had been kept. He opened the door – and sitting there, obviously waiting, was the King's mistress.

Chapter 46

He wanted to run, he wanted to stay.

Seeing his discomfort, with a light laugh, she said, 'I have not come to seduce you.'

He reddened.

'Princess Rosalie may hate me,' said the lady dismissively, 'but I have noticed I am more popular with you. Is that a fair conclusion?'

'Yes,' he said.

'You may yet hate me,' she said, 'when you hear what I have to say.'

Cadd said nothing, feeling intense discomfort. The King's mistress was in his room and he did not know how to behave. Her beauty challenged his sense – and won easily.

'Do you know I am related to Captain Loo?' she said.

'I do,' he managed to say, 'but I don't know how.'

'We are cousins. And because of him, I know more than you think.'

Cadd's heart jumped in his chest. Did she know him as an impostor? What had Loo said to her?

'We may be useful to each other, you and I,' said Lady Lula with a half smile.

He trembled, but not for her beauty. The tease was different. It was as if she were sharpening a knife, and looking at his sheeplike throat.

'How may I help you?' he said.

'You probably know,' she exclaimed, 'that there's no divorce in this country. If there were, I would be Queen by now. And I intend to be. But of course there is a certain obstacle.'

'Rosalie's mother.'

'Precisely.'

'Where do I come into this?'

She laughed, throwing her head back. 'Where do you think?'

There was no subtlety in this. He could barely believe what she was saying. It could not be other than murder. How else do you remove a reluctant wife?

'Why should I?' he said.

She held him in her blue eyes. He shivered and looked away.

'Because I know,' she said.

'Know what?' he said feebly.

'Oh, don't pretend to me,' she said. 'It ill becomes you. And I can be of so much use to you. We can work together. Do we have to be enemies? The King will do whatever I say.' She laughed. 'I know it all. From beginning to end.'

Cadd did not reply. He did not trust himself to speak – no matter what she already knew. Lady Lula held his life in her hands.

'It's little use trying to deny anything,' she said. 'I know what you have done. And I admire how you have got away with it.' She laughed. 'When is a prince not a prince? Ah, there's a riddle. I wonder what the reply is.' She searched his face. 'When he's an impostor perhaps?'

'Perhaps,' he said weakly.

It was all out. Would he have to murder for her? He sank onto a chair.

'A glass of wine perhaps,' she said. 'To calm you.'

He shook his head.

'Very well. But let's be plain. I know that you sent an impostor to do your wooing. Fine trick, I admire that. All this wooing can be very tiresome. I know, too, you had him killed.'

'Your cousin talks too much,' said Cadd as he grasped what she had just said. She took him for the real Prince. Of course. How would she know that he had survived her cousin's murder attempt?

'I doubt anyone cares about the death of the impostor,' Lula went on. 'Sound to get rid of him. But Princess Rosalie has quite a temper. I know; I have felt her anger. And if she were told an impostor was sent to woo her – what might she do?'

'Throw him in the dungeon,' suggested Cadd. 'Chop off his head.' A little more informed of this than she knew.

'And then her father – should he be informed…?' She sucked in her breath. 'Drawing and quartering would be much preferred to his punishment.'

Cadd considered. She thought him the real Prince. Telling Rosalie – that would be old news for her. But as for telling her father – oh, that was dangerous indeed. He could not deny her that. No matter who he really was.

He said, 'You want me to murder Rosalie's mother?'

She put a finger to her lips. 'Sh!'

'Would not the King do it?'

She smiled ruefully. 'There are some things even I can't get him to do. But you – you have every reason to assist me.'

'How can I trust you?'

'You have no choice,' she snapped.

'I could escape.'

'You could try. But the King will run you down. He told you of his hunting dogs. They hunt men as well as stags.'

Her ruthlessness shocked him. She was pushing him to murder. Or she would have him executed one way or another.

'I can't simply visit Rosalie's mother…and then run her through.'

'No, that would be clumsy,' she said daintily. 'But you have your soldiers. You need be nowhere near the incident…' She smiled, though it had totally lost its seductive appeal. 'But let me not give you ideas. From what my cousin tells me, you're not inexpert at these matters. You have your methods and your people, I'm sure. '

'When?' he said.

'I want it done within the week.'

Chapter 47

There was no opportunity to talk to Rosalie before the banquet, and none at the banquet either, although they sat side by side. That was no talk other than small talk because they might be overheard. They spoke of wine and music, but he could not tell her that the King's mistress had demanded that he kill Rosalie's mother. And it was the only thing he wanted to say.

But it could not be said.

Rosalie had arranged things well. There were selected guests only. One long table of them. At one end sat the King and Lady Lula. At the other sat Cadd and Rosalie. As far apart as she could get them. The betrothed couple could be honoured in toasts and speeches, but Cadd was freed from intimacy with the King or his mistress.

A great relief to him.

There were jugglers and tumblers, Bild amongst them. There were musicians, more of them than last time, playing in a group, seated on a low dais. The food had more variety; there was of course meat: venison, beef and pork – but also platters of vegetables and salad. And the wine was restricted, the goblets being smaller and not filled until well into the meal.

Although a more civilized affair, it was still difficult to talk, half the words being lost in the hubbub. There were the formal speeches, the toasts when everyone was silenced. Cadd had to make one but Rosalie had written it for him. It was short enough, lots of praise for the King and his country, thanking him for his bounty – and ending in a toast to the King of Witland. She and Cadd had gone over it in the rose garden. He waited nervously for his time to do it, but really it could not go wrong. And it did not. Everyone was on his side that evening. All the speeches sang the praises of his father, the King of Larken, and how the pending marriage of Princess Rosalie to Prince Grude would brighten the sun – or words to that effect.

During the third toast, even as he raised his goblet, Cadd reflected that if only they knew who he really was – all those knives cutting meat would be cutting him. They'd have his heart on a pole.

He could at no time forget that the Prince was returning. At that very moment on the trail. But Cadd had stolen his celebration. Stolen his betrothed. Cadd may very well be the honoured one – a minstrel was even now singing that their marriage was made in Heaven while the happy couple went around the table shaking everyone's hands – but so easily could it change in a few days.

Chapter 48

Cadd had to speak to Rosalie – but it was not to be that evening. Custom demanded they left the banquet separately: she first with her handmaidens, and then he with servants. No one was allowed to leave before them – and they were played out with betrothal music.

Once back in his rooms, he could not sleep. There was too much to think about. The Prince was on his way – and when he arrived all hell would break loose around the heads of the two Princes. And only one would survive. Added to that, if anything need be added, there was the King's mistress, who helpfully believed Cadd to be the Prince, but less helpfully insisted he kill Rosalie's mother. Lady Lula had half the story right, but that might be enough to damn all princes from Larken, real or otherwise. Should she go to the King.

And why should she not? – when he did not intend to be her assassin.

What a night! The banquet was wonderful. He was cheered to the rafters. And had his hand shaken by all the high-born in the land. All those that mattered. And all the time, riding towards Witland, came another to stake his claim. What would the King do when he arrived? And his mistress, might she yet get the other half right? To have the King and his mistress against him would be certain death.

He had Rosalie – but had been unable to speak to her. All this protocol. No wonder princes went to war.

As the horizon glowed faintly orange, he at last fell asleep. But was disturbed after an hour or so by a royal servant. He must attend the King's hunt.

The servant waited for him while he washed and put on clean clothes. He had no need to eat, being full enough from the banquet – and knowing there would be plenty on the hunt. But again, no chance to see Rosalie, for she did not come on such things. While he must; he had little enough time to impress the King. And so had to make the most of his opportunities.

Cadd was taken to the stables. Amongst the grooms was Bild. He had saddled the horse that Cadd knew from his ride to the copse. Gratefully, he mounted. And, with the other horsemen, waited for the King. There was little conversation; it was so early, all were sleepy-eyed and most the worse for wear after the banquet.

When the King arrived, he looked no better than anyone, eyes bloodshot and cursing at the grooms. He gave Cadd a perfunctory greeting, while Cadd grasped for high-born adjectives – but he need not have bothered; the King was nine-tenths asleep. And it was only his honour, as he had never missed a hunt unless on his sickbed, that had got him to the saddle.

It was all men in the hunting party – the King would not have it otherwise – riding out of the castle towards the hunting ground. They crossed the fields, the horses' hooves splattering the dew on the long grass. They stopped at a large field before a forest. Here servants had come ahead and the party, still in the saddle, were given a breakfast cup of mulled wine and fresh bread.

This cheered up the King. And that was infectious. It paid to follow the King's moods.

'I will kill a stag today!' he declared.

His huntmaster took notice. He must ensure it.

The huntmaster led them, en masse, into the forest and round about; quite where and what for, Cadd was loath to ask. It was all he could do to keep up. He was a new rider, while these gentry had been born on horseback. Though, gallantly, some of them kept back with him; he was after all an honoured son, while the King rode at the head of the party. After half an hour of charging about, Cadd made his excuse.

'I have a terrible headache.' He mimed drinking, blaming the banquet rather than his riding skills.

But some of the others were actually hungover. They had no real wish to go chasing after the King, and so were glad enough to take charge of Cadd. He followed them to the hunting lodge where they dismounted. Questions were asked of him about hunting in Larken. He had been primed on this by Loo in his training days. Yes, he hunted, as did his father the King. They had royal forests set aside for just this, where it was death for anyone to kill the King's deer.

The lodge was little more than a high platform, high enough to shelter underneath, should it rain. And walled, except at the front facing the hunting ground. The party went up to the top. There, laid out on a long table, was meat, bread and wine. And they sat on benches, drinking and eating – waiting for the King to kill his stag.

And at last he came onto the hunting field before them, followed by his party. He was carrying a spear at shoulder height. From the other end, a stag was being driven by dogs and beaters on foot. The creature had no choice but to run towards the King as the dogs came for it. The King waited his moment.

And skilfully, the deer was driven perhaps five yards from him. The King threw his spear. And obviously had some art at this, as it struck the deer in its flank. Whether it might have killed the animal or not was not left to chance. A dozen arrows followed and the animal, more and more crippled, fell at last in a heap.

The King rode to the fallen creature. He dismounted. And with several slashes of a large blade, held up the antlered head. From all around, a great cheer went up. The

King tossed the head to his servants, remounted and galloped to the hunting lodge.

There, still bloodied, he joined them at the feast. All were full of praise for his prowess. Cadd joined in – that was why he had come. The King took the compliments as of right. He ate, he drank – and then, as promised, took Cadd to see his dogs.

They were various. Smaller dogs, larger dogs, dogs for hunting different animals. Cadd was out of his depth here and somewhat uncomfortable. He would be expected to know something about dogs, whereas he knew nothing. But found it best to ask questions which the King and the huntmaster were pleased enough to answer. Simple questions – which is your favourite, which is the best stag hunter, how many hounds do you have, how often do you hunt…

Nevertheless, when the morning was over, he was exhausted. It was hard work being so in view and constantly aware of his own ignorance. He returned to his rooms, changed out of his hunting clothes, and went to see Rosalie.

She was with her handmaidens, doing embroidery. On his arrival, she clapped her hands and asked them all to leave her. And they were at once away.

'How was the hunt?' she said.

'Your father killed a stag,' he said.

'He always does. Did you see his dogs?'

'Every puppy and bitch.'

She laughed. But he had not come to simply chat.

'Last night,' he said, 'I had a visit.'

'Who?'

'Lady Lula.'

'Another bitch,' she said. 'What did she want of you?'

'To kill your mother.'

Rosalie's eyes widened. 'I'm not surprised at her thinking; surprised, though, she picked you. Why?'

'Captain Loo is her cousin.'

'The one who tried to kill you?'

'Yes, him.'

'So what did he tell her?'

'That an impostor came to woo you. But the impostor is now dead.'

Rosalie laughed. 'Well at least you have fooled her. She thinks you are the true Prince, my love. And she has some influence, you may have noticed, on my father.'

'Unless I kill your mother in a week, she will inform your father that I sent an impostor to woo you.'

Rosalie fell about laughing. She waved her hands in her helplessness.

Cadd watched her incredulously. 'Is it really so funny?'

She calmed herself. 'No, not so funny. I hardly know why I laughed. Just the thought of her getting it so wrong. And picking you to do her dirty work. Of all people.'

'She says if she tells the King the truth, then he'll kill me. Is that so?'

She thought about this. 'Probably. Though not for certain. He'll be very offended of course. But you do have me. And I don't want him to kill you.'

'Thank you for that.'

'Ten years in the dungeon will do.' She kissed him on the cheek.

'I've seen the dungeon. I wouldn't last a year.'

Rosalie was biting her finger thoughtfully. 'She may have miscalculated. If it were my father and me against you — well, that would be the end of you. Goodbye. But it isn't. I am for you. And he has paraded you, taken you hunting. So he won't want to give you up if he can help it.' She paused thoughtfully. 'I think with me on your side and you begging his forgiveness – he would forgive you.'

'Can you be sure of that?'

She shrugged. 'Not when it comes to that bitch.' She stopped and rethought. 'But I'd put money on it. I will plead for you. You will be a good husband. So why risk a war?'

'Even to please a mistress?'

'I don't think she'll push that hard,' she said. 'Think about it. What has she to gain by your death? By my mother's death – the bitch becomes Queen. But yours? What does she gain? My father would simply arrange another round of suitors. Heaven help me there. But nothing to serve her ends.'

'I'm so glad I spoke to you.'

'Come here,' she said.

He sat by her on the sofa. She laid her head on his shoulder.

'I think we can beat her,' she mused.

'But what if she were to side with the Prince when he arrives?'

'Then all bets are off,' she said lightly.

Chapter 49

The next day, Bild came to see him.

'The Prince has been seen,' he said.

'When will he arrive?'

'Our messenger says in about three hours.'

Cadd clapped his hands to his head. 'Heavens! I am scared stiff, Bild.'

'It's dangerous for all of us. The King knows nothing,' said Bild.

Cadd shivered. 'Just three hours. Who will meet him?'

'Princess Rosalie is sending out a dozen of her men to bring them in. They will believe it is an advance guard to welcome them...'

'And it isn't?' queried Cadd.

'No. When they arrive at the castle, his troop will be asked to camp outside. As soon as he enters he will be arrested.'

'And then what?'

'The King will be told that a man impersonating the Prince has entered the castle...'

Cadd sat silently for a minute. It was all happening so quickly. The first part, at least, planned out. He had no part to play – but knew it would not go on that way. The Prince would not meekly be arrested. Loo would likely be with him. And – the lady, his cousin, he knew she would come into it.

'What will the King do?' he said.

'I can't be sure,' said Bild, 'but I think he will want to see the two of you. And after that...' He stopped and shrugged.

'May the best liar win,' said Cadd.

Bild smiled grimly and said, 'Princess Rosalie says, stay in your rooms. Let things take their course. You will be called for.'

The dwarf turned to go.

'Thank you, Bild.'

'Don't thank me yet. Reward me if you have a head on your shoulders tomorrow.'

Chapter 50

Over the next few hours, Cadd went to his window regularly. He had a good view of the courtyard. And saw the usual business of a large castle: servants running here and there, maids, boys, men in livery, soldiers going on and off duty, dignitaries in and out of their offices, wagons entering and leaving... All the day to day traffic.

Nothing unusual.

And then he saw Princess Rosalie. She was coming into the courtyard off the drawbridge with a party of soldiers. She and six soldiers were on horseback; the rest, following, were on foot. He counted the foot soldiers, about thirty, all with pikes. The captain busied himself positioning the men on either side of the gate – so they might not be seen until whoever, he knew quite well who, was in the courtyard.

Cadd was agitated and could not stay still. He knew it could not be long before the Prince arrived. She had not told the King yet, and so would want to keep this preparation to a minimum. And so it proved.

The Prince and Loo rode into the courtyard laughing together. They were followed by twelve of Rosalie's men on horseback. Immediately, the pikemen jumped out. Loo drew his sword, but the twelve horsemen behind drew theirs. Loo shook his head and put his sword away. The Prince was shouting, but Cadd could not make out his words. Rosalie, who was on horseback to one side, yelled something, and the Prince was dragged off his horse. Loo dismounted voluntarily. And they were led off by the party of pikemen. Cadd could not see where they were going. He suspected the dungeon – but could not see far enough round.

It had happened. So quickly. A minute perhaps, no more. And the courtyard was back to business.

Chapter 51

Rosalie came for him.

'This is it,' she said.

He had been expecting the call, and left immediately with her. As they crossed the courtyard, she said, 'I am coming in with you. Arm in arm. I shall be your support.'

'I need all I can get.'

He was shaking. He had to face the King, Loo and the Prince, and claim he was the true Prince.

'Stop,' she said, and held him back. 'Breathe slowly.'

He rested on his stick. 'I shall die of nerves,' he said.

'Don't imagine the Prince is so happy,' she said. 'He's been arrested and thrown in the dungeon. No one has told him why. When you walk into the room it will hit him hard. He has been told you're dead. And there you are – as alive as he is. At least you've thought about your lies. He's not prepared. He didn't know he had to be.'

'Only one of us will come out of this alive.'

She kissed him on the cheek. 'It will be you,' she said.

He could not feel her certainty. And doubted she really felt it. He must outface the Prince who had chained him, trained him, used him and then tried to drown him.

'Let's go for him,' he said, steeling himself. 'I want to see his face as I enter the room.'

She took his arm and led him to a door he had never entered before. A guard stood to one side. He saluted them and opened it. They walked in arm in arm.

Inside were two soldiers at the rear; before them were the King, Lady Lula, both seated and Loo and the Prince standing. Grude and Loo blanched as Cadd entered. They looked to each other startled. And well they might, as their fates were entwined. The Prince was dishevelled by his hours in the dungeon – and smelt rather pungently, a smell Cadd remembered too well.

Cadd smiled wryly at Grude. The shock of the Prince had given him courage. The Prince would make mistakes. His own time had come. He must be the Prince.

'Your Majesty,' said Cadd bowing. 'Your ladyship,' he said to Lula. 'I have been told there is an impersonator here. And I can well see who it is.'

'A good copy indeed,' said Lula.

'I am Prince Grude,' exclaimed Grude. 'He is an impostor.'

'How dare you!' shouted Cadd and slapped Grude round the face.

Grude went to hit him back but was immediately grasped by soldiers.

'I am Prince Grude,' yelled Grude, the guards holding his arms, looking to the others in hurt appeal. 'I have come from Larken to claim my betrothed.'

'I am already claimed, whoever you are,' snapped Rosalie.

'Quiet!' shouted the King. 'I cannot deal with all these voices.'

The room was silenced.

'Let him go, guards.' The soldiers released Grude. The King rose from his seat and paced before the two claimants. He stared them keenly in the eye, looking for a flinch. 'There are two of you here,' he went on, 'both claiming to be the Prince of Larken.' His eyes went from one to the other. 'The likeness is incredible. The hair, the eyes, both with sticks even. But one of you is lying. And that one will die.'

He walked up to Grude and held him firmly by the shoulders.

'Who are you?'

'I am Prince Grude.'

'Who are you really?'

'I am Prince Grude.'

The King walked up to Cadd and gripped him by the shoulders.

'Who are you?'

'I am Prince Grude, Your Majesty.'

'Who are you really?'

'I am Prince Grude, Your Majesty.'

The King smiled. 'We have a delightful puzzle here.' He turned to Rosalie. 'Which of these is Prince Grude, my dear?'

She walked up to Cadd and took his arm. 'He is.'

'What do you say to that?' said the King to the dishevelled Prince.

'She is mistaken, Your Majesty. He is very like me and she has made an error.' He looked to Rosalie. 'I beg your pardon, Your Highness.'

'Mistakes can be made,' said the King. 'Lula, my love – who do you think is the Prince?'

'I have a sense for liars,' she said. She crossed to Cadd and smiled sweetly at him. Then went to Grude. She held her fingers to her lips contemplatively. 'They are so very good,' she said.

'But which one is the Prince?' said the King.

'Him.' She pointed to Grude.

'She's lying,' yelled Rosalie. 'Getting at me.'

'Quiet, my dear,' said the King. 'This is not over yet.'

He crossed to Loo.

'Captain Loo. You are related, I hear, to Lady Lula.'

'She is my cousin, Your Majesty.'

'I see the likeness. Now tell me – which of these two young men is the Prince?'

Cadd swallowed. Lula was against him and Loo certainly had no love for him. Rosalie, by his side, squeezed his hand. Did she feel as desperate as he did?

'Your Majesty,' said Loo, 'I can't say which.'

The King looked at him startled. 'But didn't you ride in with this one?'

'I did, Your Majesty. And I can tell them apart now because they are wearing different clothing. But if I saw him,' he pointed out Grude, 'on his own – I would say he was the Prince. And if I saw him,' pointing out Cadd, 'I would say he was the Prince.'

Cadd thought – what is he playing at? And it came to him as Lula glared at Loo. Loo was opting for the winning side, and wasn't yet sure which it would be.

Grude yelled, 'Loo, tell them! You know the truth. You rode with me from Larken!'

'I met you part way,' declared Loo. 'You may have come from Larken. You may not have done.'

'I came from Larken,' screamed Grude.

'Quiet,' said the King. 'Or you will be removed.' He turned to Cadd. 'What have you to say to Captain Loo?'

'Thank you, Your Majesty,' said Cadd. To Loo he said, 'When I came to woo Rosalie – you came with me.'

Loo smiled. 'I came with one of you. But I really can't say which.'

What is he doing, thought Cadd. He will not say for either of us.

'Ask him a question,' ordered Lula of Grude.

Grude looked to the King, who nodded.

He said to Cadd, 'How many castles has my father?'

'*My* father has seven,' said Cadd.

Grude scowled.

'What is the answer?' said the King.

'Seven,' hissed Grude.

'Ask him another,' said Lula.

'My turn,' interjected Cadd.

The King nodded.

Cadd bit his lip and gazed at Grude; he could feel his intense anger. He was like a chained lion; Grude would tear him to pieces if he could.

He said, 'You have come here, you say, to claim your betrothed.'

'Yes,' said Grude.

'You were here a week ago to win her.'

'I was.'

'You were one of three Princes...'

'Yes.'

'This is a lot of questioning,' protested Lula.

'Let him continue,' said the King. 'There has been no real question yet. Ask it, now.'

Cadd bowed, 'Yes, Your Majesty. I was preparing the ground.' He turned back to Grude. 'Three tests were set to win Princess Rosalie. What were they?'

Grude looked wildly about him. Then to Loo. Cadd knew that Loo would know, but the Captain made no sign.

'What was the first?' said the King.

Grude desperately thrust at his temple. 'Riding,' he exclaimed.

The King turned to Cadd. 'What was it?'

'We had a race,' said Cadd.

'Yes, you did,' said the King smiling wryly at the claimants. 'And that is riding. Both correct.' Still with Cadd he said, 'And what was the second?'

'Archery,' said Cadd. 'I did very badly.'

'You did,' said the King, nodding in approval. He turned to Grude. 'And the third test?'

Grude was breathing heavily, looking around for help. Loo, who could, was hardly able to assist in this searching company. Grude was on his own. Did he know, or did he not? How much had Loo told him of the time?

'I've... forgotten,' he said.

'It was not so long ago,' said the King impatiently. 'Try.'

Grude sucked his fist and moved from foot to foot. A low groan slipped from his lips. His neck rested on the answer. Cadd clenched his fist and hoped that the Prince and Loo had been sloppy in their preparation.

The Prince shook himself. He said, 'My father's illness, my coming betrothal... The riding back and forth. And the shock of arrest and being thrown in the dungeon...'

'Answer!' roared the King.

Grude was pushed back by the force of it. The words on his lips died.

Instead, he said meekly, 'Diving, Your Majesty.'

Cadd was smashed by disappointment. They had prepared. Damn them. On the journey here, Loo and he must have talked it through. Cadd needed another question. Something Loo could not tell him.

'And what do you think was the last task?' said the King to Cadd.

'We dived for a ring,' said Cadd. 'I won that test.'

Rosalie rounded on Grude. 'Whose ring was it?'

'Yours,' he said. 'It belonged to your mother. It had a large red stone.'

Rosalie cursed. 'He has been schooled!'

'Restrain your outbursts,' said the King. 'We have two here – both well schooled. And I have no wish to execute both.

Cadd was thinking, he could ask Grude about the time he spent with Rosalie. But then who could confirm that but Rosalie – and she was already for him. He needed to persuade the King.

'Who,' yelled Grude, 'is my mother's youngest brother's wife?'

'It is not his turn,' exclaimed Rosalie.

'Perhaps not,' said Lula, the voice of sweet reason, 'but it is a testing question. One I would like answered. After all, a Prince should know his own family. Is that not so, Sire?'

And she smiled at the King. A smile he returned.

'Answer the question,' said the King to Cadd.

Cadd was in desperation. He did not recall the answer. Perhaps had never known it. Yes, he'd been taken through the Prince's family. And he knew the Prince's mother's brothers. But their wives...? He was standing on quicksand.

'He has him!' yelled Lula. She was off her chair, her skirts shaking in her delight. 'See how he trembles. See the fear in his eye. Admit you are the liar!'

'Stop her, Father,' shouted Rosalie. 'Why she is here at all – I do not know.'

'Perhaps because I am a better judge than you are, my dear.'

'At judging your own advantage,' hissed Rosalie.

The King swung an arm in a wide arc. 'One more word from either and you shall be removed.' He turned to Cadd. 'Can you answer the question?'

Cadd shook his head. 'She is a minor relative, Your Majesty. I have not seen her in ages...'

The King addressed Loo. 'Write down who it is.'

Loo went to the desk where there was a quill and ink. He wrote. The only sound in the room the scratching of the pen. Loo savoured his moments of complete attention. Without rushing, he blotted the ink, then folded the paper which he handed to the King.

'Your Majesty.' Loo bowed.

Cadd looked to Rosalie. She was crushed. And no wonder – there was no assistance she could give him in knowing the full life of the Prince. There were too many checks that could be made. The detail was beyond him. He should have ridden off when he could. Love had blinded him. He was doomed.

'Who is…' began the King addressing Grude. He stopped with the flap of his hand. 'Which relative was it?'

'My mother's youngest brother's wife, Your Majesty,' said Grude.

'So who is she?'

'Lady Erl,' said Grude, with a broad smile and a bow.

The King opened the paper.

'It is she,' he said. He turned to Cadd. 'Why are you so ill informed on your relatives?' Cadd could not reply, nor hold the King's eye. 'Shall we go through more of them?'

Cadd shook his head. It would be useless. There was only one here for him – and she was as helpless as he was.

The King snapped his fingers. 'Take him away, guards.'

The soldiers rapidly crossed the room and grasped Cadd by the arms.

'There will only be one Prince of Larken in my kingdom,' said the King. 'And the impostor shall hang in the morning.'

Chapter 52

The others had gone. Two remained.

Rosalie stood before her father, head bowed.

'Spare him, Father,' she said.

The King gazed over her head, a pillar of immobility in his long green cloak, his arms on his thick waist, buttresses to his fixity.

'I cannot,' he said.

'Please,' she pleaded. And dropped to her knees at his feet.

The King shook his head.

'I will not allow impostors,' he said.

She tugged at his cloak the way she had done as an infant. 'He was put up to it, Father. Prince Grude forced him to come and to woo me.'

'How can you believe anything from that proven liar?' said the King angrily.

'I do believe him,' she said. 'Father – he is good. He was forced into this.'

'Forced?' said the King turning his back on her. 'Even should I believe the story that he came to woo you, coerced by Prince Grude... Why did he then return and pretend he was the real Prince?'

'It was my advice, Father.' Her head sank to the stones of the floor. 'I was wrong, Father. I should have told him to ride away and never return. Instead, I said he should come and have my hand...' She stopped and raised her head. 'Blame me.'

'I cannot believe your foolishness.' He stood over her as if she were a dog. 'You – a princess of the realm, attempting by such subterfuge to raise a commoner to princely rank...' He flailed for words. 'It is disgusting, you make me sick.'

'Should your disgust of me – take his life, Father?'

He lowered himself to her level and took her face in both hands.

'He will die,' he said firmly. 'Already I have shamed the Kingdom by arresting Prince Grude. His father is powerful and his hours in my dungeon could even lead to war. I have no choice. I must execute this impostor. And give my profoundest apologies to Prince Grude for his humiliation on his arrival.'

'It is all my fault,' she said. 'Please spare him. I beg of you.'

He pushed her backwards and rose. 'You don't listen to your father. I cannot spare him. The only voice I would listen to would be Prince Grude's. Should he ask – then I would be merciful. But you are already condemned in this.'

'Please, Father...'

'Stop! Don't beg me like a peasant girl. Your mother made me feeble with you. I have given in too often and I will not this time. There can be but one remedy. The impostor is exposed. I will not be seen as a weak king. He must die. He must be seen to die.'

'Father...' she began.

'Enough!' He pointed to the door. 'Go to your room.'

She rose, head drooping. Beaten.

'He will hang,' said the King, the audience at an end. 'And you will marry Prince Grude.'

Chapter 53

He was chained to the wall by his ankles, and also by his hands at waist height. The shortness of the chains on his hands meant he could not sit down, nor even get his knees to the ground. His discomfort had been added to by his visitors. Cadd had only been in the dungeon perhaps an hour when Loo and Prince Grude came. Loo had beaten him up and asked permission to kill him there and then. This had been refused, as the Prince insisted that Cadd must be hanged in the morning. And further more, the beating must be limited so that he could walk to the gallows. Loo stuck more or less to the limits imposed by his Prince, his enjoyment reduced – but he agreed with the Prince that there was no pleasure to be had in seeing a man hang who did not even know of it.

They had taken off his boots. They were not far off, simply out of reach in his chained circumstance. Not that he could see them in the dungeon light, or that it would matter much to him if he could. Cadd was forced to stand on his one foot and the pain of it had become excruciating. He was battered and bruised from his beating, dried blood caked about his face, chest and arms. A bone in his shoulder was dislocated, which made any comfort hopeless. It was only possible to take the weight off his foot by taking it on the chains on his arms – and with a dislocated shoulder arm, this could hardly be done.

Pain took over completely. He could not think who he was, who he'd been, of relatives alive or dead. Or even of Rosalie. And there was no future to think of. He pulsated with agony. In the darkness a red wall was before his eyes that moved back and forth to the spasms of his suffering. If there was any thought – it was reduced to this simplicity: he was to die and he wanted it over.

Outside, there was hammering and sawing. The carpenters were assembling the gibbet: making the platform and assembling the uprights. They must complete their work before it grew late, for then there would be complaints from the ladies and gentlemen at having their sleep disturbed. They worked by lamplight, but it was an easy enough task – the wooden pieces had been stacked away from the last hanging. A few needed replacing; most of the others simply had to be nailed or bolted in place. There were four carpenters, they had done this before – and should have it completed in an hour.

Later, Loo returned to the dungeon, alone this time. He was half drunk and insulted Cadd and punched him – but soon stopped as he was disappointed in getting so little response. He gave up after a few more kicks and slaps, wondering whether he had gone too far. But would anyone really care if the mudfish couldn't walk to the gallows in the morning?

This was not a question that had any meaning for Cadd himself, who was beyond considering. He had fallen into a stupor, the pain too much for his body to bear, hanging like a slab of meat on his chains.

Chapter 54

'I deeply beg your pardon,' said Rosalie, as she curtseyed before him as he entered her chambers. 'It is to my shame that I ever doubted you, Prince Grude.'

He said, waving a hand, 'It was a natural mistake.'

She led him to the sofa, where he sat down. She presented him with a goblet of wine, taking one herself. He sipped his wine, feeling completely in command. He would make her pay after marriage. She deserved it for her ugliness alone. Her hunchback – why had no one told him? Even Loo had kept it from him. One of his damn jokes. Another who'd pay. He had some scores yet to settle.

And still, she was flattering and curtseying. Every time she dropped to her knees he saw that back. Would she never stop? Did she not realise that it was best to hide that feature? Her face was acceptable. It was the back. Like a great mountain. Was he really expected to be seen in company with one so deformed? He – the Prince of Larken. Give it a few months and he'd teach her her place. He'd take his model from her father, the King. In fact, why not send his wife to live with the King's wife? The thought made him smirk. Mother and daughter reunited. And – the idea occurred to him – why not in a year or so – dispose of the daughter entirely? But even so, the thought of twelve months' marriage – to that. He shuddered, and hid it in a slurp of wine.

He needed his drink tonight. All these interviews. First that trial with the King, and now this goblin who he must marry. And be pleasant to, at least until the ceremony was over. Then he'd take her back to Larken, and teach her who was her master.

He laughed into his mug. She thought she was attractive to him. That ridiculous dress hid nothing. And see how she was smiling and flirting with him. He'd have her hidden behind a curtain, in closed rooms. Suppose they had a child, born like that? The thought shook him: a baby with a hunchback. He'd have it killed. He wouldn't live surrounded by gnomes.

And yet she had dared denounce him. He would punish her for picking the wrong side. Grude did not forgive. He considered it not a virtue, but cowardly. Something that women did.

She said, 'Prince Grude, I know you are not the one that came to woo me.'

He smiled at her, wine dripping down his chin. This did not surprise him now. Obviously, it was why she had clung to the baker's boy.

'Do you mind?' he said.

'It was rather mischievous,' she said.

Maybe, he thought, but he could never have wooed such a creature. How clever of him to have sent the baker's boy. It was Loo's stupidity that had nearly ruined it.

He said, 'Will you tell your father?'

'It depends.' She laughed lightly. 'You see, although you look alike – you are not alike.'

'True.'

'And so I made my promise to someone else... Do I now have to keep it?'

His hand went to his mouth as he thought out the implications. He didn't want to marry her, but his father wanted him to. There were treaties, castles, land in this. Good reasons. But why the hell did it have to be him!

He said, 'You're not quite my sort.'

And wished he hadn't – but too late, it was said. And why shouldn't she know?

She said, 'Nor you mine.'

That offended him. To be told by this rook's carrion that she considered herself too good for him. That was an affront she would pay for.

'If I told my father that you had sent a double to woo me – he would be very angry.'

Grude smiled wryly. 'He would not believe you.'

'Suppose I had the impostor tortured?' she retorted.

Grude shook his head. 'He is barely alive now. He can tell you nothing.'

'Barely alive, you say?'

'I considered he deserved a night of agony for his affront.'

He watched the tears welling in her eyes. Damn the woman, he thought – she weeps for my copy. She supported the fake; she says I am not her sort. And she's ugly as a rat. There are hard lessons to be taught. And it would give me greatest pleasure to be her instructor.

'Let's marry,' he said cheerfully. 'We can make it work.'

'If we are agreed,' she said, 'that it is for the betterment of our kingdoms. And not for love.'

He grinned. 'I'm glad we understand each other.'

'Then let's drink to our marriage,' she said.

They both raised their goblets. And drank.

Suddenly the Prince was laughing uncontrollably. The drink had hit him.

'Do you know that woman... what's her name...' he was snapping his fingers. 'Lady Lula – her with the bedroom eyes... We had a talk in the courtyard when we left your father. Do you know what she wants me to do?' He was giggling now. It was all so funny.

'Do tell me?'

'Kill your mother.'

He was bent double in his laughter. It was all so ridiculous. Doubles and mistresses and princesses with hunchbacks... He was howling with mirth.

'Will you?' she said sweetly.

He flapped his hands; speaking was so difficult. The room was wobbly. How things were shaking!

He managed to say, 'Better not. Not now I've told you.' And was laughing again. Clutching his stomach. He really could not stop.

She said, 'Unless you kill me too.'

And he might have noted that she was not smiling, but he was too swept away in his laughter. The room was swimming in and out of focus. Her head, growing larger and smaller. And her hunchback, mountainous... And the next thought came out in speech but he did not know it:

'You must have goats running up and down your back!'

For he was rapidly losing consciousness, the laughter dying as he clutched his stomach and flailed the air. And then he was gone, mouth wide open, head resting on the sofa back.

She watched, gave him perhaps half a minute. The drug had done its work. Though she wondered at one moment. It seemed to be taking an age. And then she wished it had slowed – when he had started talking of Lula's plan. The content was of no surprise to her; it was just the fact that Lula had homed in on Grude so quickly. Whichever Prince was in the ascendant.

Rosalie picked up her embroidery bag. She placed it on the sofa – and removed from it a knife. She jerked Grude's head over the top of the sofa by his hair, pulled out his tongue and hacked at it. She was halfway through when he woke for an instant, gurgled with the blood in his mouth, thrashed with both arms and fell back into a swoon. She completed the slicing – and placed the fat, leaf-like piece on the low table. His mouth was bubbling like a fountain. She had no wish for him to drown and so pushed him over, face down – and the blood rushed out into the fabric of the seat.

She took out a pair of knitting needles from her bag. Standing over him, she stabbed one into each ear. The first pulled out easily, the second stuck – and she had to use both hands to draw it out, bloody with fibres of flesh along its length.

Princess Rosalie placed the needles and knife by the tongue on the table, and walked to the door. She glanced back at the Prince lying face down on the sofa, blood dripping from his mouth like a leaky gutter. One hand was on the low table, inches from the tongue piece, as if he sought to reclaim it; the other, covering one ear, with blood seeping through the fingers.

She opened the door. And put her head alone outside, her hands too gory to be exposed.

'Tell the King he must come at once,' she ordered. 'Prince Grude is in trouble.'

Chapter 55

'You shall hang for this.' The King held up the flap of tongue carefully between finger and thumb. 'The gibbet is erected. It can take two as easily as one.'

'Hang me then,' she said defiantly, 'and see where that gets you.'

'You disgrace me.' He put down the tongue, distastefully. 'You are no better than your mother!'

'But am I worse than my father?'

The King was in his dressing gown. He stared in disbelief at the Prince who was now awake, laid out on the sofa and alternatively clutching at his mouth and ears, gurgling and groaning.

'This will mean war,' said the King, unable to keep his eyes off the apparition, running his hands through his wiry hair.

The sofa was stained in blood. His daughter's dress was like a butcher's apron.

'No, Father, it doesn't have to mean war.'

'He can't go back to Larken without a tongue...'

'He will not.'

The King could not take his eyes off the bubbling blood. That was the Prince of Larken... He turned away with a grimace.

'Explain yourself, child.'

'We have a Prince. With a tongue.'

'I do not understand you...' He stopped, then understood in a rush. 'We have a likeness.' He shook his head. 'It can't be done.'

'Will you send a tongueless Prince back to Larken then?'

The King walked around the chamber shaking his head. 'No, no, impossible.' He waved his hands wildly about, his eyes drawn back to the groaning Prince. 'See what you have done? There will be war. Even if I execute you, it will be unforgivable. We are not ready for war. We may lose everything for this stupidity...'

'Father. Do as I say. It will not mean war.'

'What have you done?' the King exclaimed, held by the bloody mouth: within, a ragged end in a well of frothing red.

Rosalie stood between him and Grude. She gripped his forearms in her stained hands.

'You must execute this one,' she commanded. 'And I will marry the other.'

The King pushed her away. 'Should it ever be revealed? Then what?'

'Then there will be war,' she said quietly. 'No worse than now. But should it not be – then we have peace, and the bringing together of the kingdoms.'

'How did you get me to this hell?' moaned the King, his hands pulling at his hair.

'*He* got us here,' she declared, pointing to the gurgling body, 'when he sent a double to woo me.'

Her father flapped a hand in vexation. 'Not that again.'

'Believe me once,' she exclaimed. 'Do you think I cannot know?'

'It barely matters,' said the King. He straightened himself. 'What is done is done. I cannot send *that* back on a stretcher. And I don't wish to hang you – though you well deserve it.' He had resumed statesman mode, shock over – or as over as it could be, with the spluttering Prince on the sofa. 'I cannot leave him alive,' he continued. 'He has heard too much.'

'He hears nothing,' she said. 'I have stabbed his ears.'

The King gazed at her in horror, tinged with admiration. 'You are surely my daughter. I feared after I was gone, the kingdom might be lost... But you will not flinch.'

'No, Father.'

'We must remove this bloody mess – and bring up the other.' He did not move though, riveted by the thrashing and choking Grude, the eyes wide, appealing. The King jerked away and snapped his fingers at a thought. 'Loo. His captain. He will cause us trouble.'

'I've had him arrested, Father.'

He half smiled. 'Good. You have thought this out. But suppose I had disagreed with your action?'

'And sewn Grude's tongue back on, Father? And given him your ears?'

The King pulled at his beard. 'You are cunning, Rosalie. A few hours ago, you begged at my knee – a veritable wailing wretch. And when that didn't work…' He stretched an arm before the gruesome tableau. 'You did this. Which gives me no choice.' He sighed. 'I should hang you. Truly. But this is pretty work. In its way.' He turned from it. 'Let it be.'

Grude grabbed at the King's gown. He pushed him away in disgust and Grude fell back, his hands rushing to his gory mouth.

'Let it be,' repeated the King.

Chapter 56

Loo had escaped.

While being taken down the stairs to the dungeon, he had swung on his guards, grabbed a spear – killed one and driven the other down the stairs. He then raced to the stables and was away before the alarm could be called.

The King, alerted, sent his men in pursuit.

In darkness, Cadd was brought up from the dungeon to his bed. He lay unconscious, Rosalie at his bedside ministering with the healer to his wounds. Prince Grude in turn was carried down to the same dungeon. There was no need for shackles. He was thrown in the cell and the door slammed shut. All night he groaned and thrashed in the damp straw. He had no words, and for sound heard only the hissing in his ears.

Early in the morning, he was taken out for the hanging. He could not walk, his head was swollen and bulging, a reddened ball of pus and pain – and he had to be assisted by two soldiers. He was not recognizable; in truth, more dead than alive. It was a disappointing hanging. Grude had to be held on the gibbet while the necessary actions were carried out. There was no struggle in him, but a constant gurgle which may have been an attempt at a plea or simply agony.

There were quite a few up to watch even at this early hour. Hangings were normally later, but the King wanted this over quickly. He came himself, Rosalie watched from Cadd's window. The hangman placed the noose over Grude's head. He was lifted to the stool by soldiers, held there while the hangman adjusted the noose. The priest asked if he had any last words. He hadn't. And the hangman pulled the stool away. The weight of the body tightened the rope, the neck jerked as the spinal cord snapped, the legs kicking in a short spasm – and it was over.

The crowd waited; sometimes there was an after-spasm. But this one had given in quickly. There wasn't much to talk about over breakfast. The fake prince had snuffed it – finish your porridge and go about your work.

'Long live the Prince,' sighed Rosalie.

Grude was cut down half an hour later. He was bundled in a sack, an irony Cadd might have appreciated if he had been awake. Then taken away on a wagon accompanied by five soldiers. His last entourage took him to the King's forest a mile or so away. And there a large bonfire was built – and before it was lit, the bundle placed on top. And then set ablaze.

It took several hours for the body to burn completely. The fire had to be fed to keep it roaring hot. Onlookers were kept away as the body fried in its own fat. Blood and water boiled off, and finally the dried flesh burnt. A guard was kept there all day, and then through the night.

The next morning, the embers were raked over for remnants: pieces of bone, a buckle, pins. Any fragment of body or clothing that might be recognised. These bits were taken deeper into the forest and buried six feet deep.

Chapter 57

Cadd awoke after two days.

'Hello,' he said, blinking in the new light.

'Hello,' she replied, amused at his bewilderment.

'I'm not dead – am I?'

She smiled gently at his lack of certainty. 'You are alive. Mind you, someone who looked a little like you has recently died.'

'Who?'

'No one important. A former prince.'

'Grude?'

'Of course not. You are Grude,' she said. 'Remember?'

'I am Grude,' he said with hesitation. 'Yes, I am. Of course. But this former prince – what happened to him?'

'He was a fake,' she said. 'Confirmed. Tried to copy you. How dare he! So we hanged him. And burnt him. And buried the bits that were left.' She kissed Cadd on the cheek. 'And that's what happens to fakes.'

'Fakes are a nuisance,' he said. And then added, 'I don't know how you managed it.'

'I won't give you details. You won't like it. But you were right. He was rather unpleasant.'

'A beast,' said Cadd.

'Then perhaps it was right to butcher him,' she mused. 'How do you feel?'

'Stiff,' he said. 'I hurt all over. Loo beat me up... I remember that. Almost the last thing I do remember.'

'Yes, Loo,' she pondered. 'He's escaped. See – it's not just you who can do it.'

'Is he still dangerous?'

'Yes, but could be worse. He got away before the change-over, so he thinks you are hanged. Father believes that Grude, I mean not you, the other one, the beast...

This is muddling. Anyway, Father says that Loo thinks the beast had him arrested for doubting him. Whether that's so or not, we don't believe he has gone back to Larken. But just in case, Father has sent a messenger to the King of Larken to say that Loo is a traitor and tried to attack the Prince. You. The one who is not a beast.'

'Damn Loo.' Another thought struck him. 'What of his lovely cousin?'

'Oh, as nauseating as ever. But without Loo she is somewhat neutered. Though we must keep an eye on her.'

'This is a rough world.'

'Then thank heaven that you have me,' she said. 'You will always have enemies now you are the Prince.'

He felt somewhat overwhelmed in the waking world. All that had taken place while he slept... He relapsed into a simplicity as valid for princes as for bakers' sons.

'I'm hungry,' he said.

'Oh, good,' she said clapping her hands. 'That means you are on the mend. We are to be married in three weeks.'

'Why so soon?' On seeing her widened eyes, he continued, 'I'm not complaining – just that's hardly time for the relatives from Larken to get here...' quietly he added, 'some of whom I haven't even met.'

'That's the very point,' she said. 'The fewer that come the better. Rush wedding. And Father says, those that come he'll keep busy. Hunts, banquets, boating...' She stopped. 'Anyone you want to invite?'

He shook his head. Everyone had gone.

'Just you,' he said.

'I'll do my best to come,' she said lightly, 'if I'm not too busy.' She smoothed his brow. 'Oh, I'm so glad – you're back. It was awful when I thought you were going to be hanged.'

'I'm still hungry,' he said.

'I'll see about that...' She rose.

'After I've eaten, will you do something for me?'

'I might. I might not.'

'Will you bathe my stump?'

'Of course,' she smiled. 'And then my back... It still remembers your fingers. Do you think...?'

'Always,' he said. 'I am your Prince.'

Chapter 58

In three weeks, Cadd and Rosalie were married. In the interim, as soon as he was well enough, Cadd and she went riding every day.

'You must ride like a prince,' she said. 'Not like a baker.'

She taught him archery. And, when he could at last hit the target, handed him over to a tutor. She did the same with reading and writing, though from all accounts, the Prince, the old one, had not been so good himself. Slightly better than Cadd, so he had a little catching up to do. Amongst the Prince's things were found his seal and samples of his handwriting. This is what Cadd found most arduous, learning to write like the Prince. But this he must do for communications with Larken. He copied and copied – and his hand in the end grew sufficiently like the Prince's for it to escape comment.

The marriage went smoothly. There were about thirty guests from Larken. As they arrived, they were carefully questioned by the King's servants about their relationship to Prince Grude. The guests were informed it was for the seating plan at the banquet – but in reality it was so that Cadd should know who was who. And, as planned, the relatives were kept busy with hunts, dances, excursions on the river so as to have only cursory chats with Cadd while on the run from event to event. And of course, Cadd and Rosalie had to go and see her mother just after the wedding.

Cadd sent for news of his parents, and incredibly they were still alive. Grude had meant to kill them, but it was not important to him, and could have been arranged easily when he got back. Except, of course, he never got back. Cadd's mother, his father and Jel, his brother, were in a dungeon in a remote castle. He had them freed and taken back to the town of Tolga. They were given money to set up anew – but were not told who was their benefactor. How could he tell them? The Prince could not also be a baker's son. Besides, it was dangerous for his parents and brother to know the truth. One day, perhaps, when he was secure, he would let himself be known – but he was far from secure yet. This troubled him terribly, but he knew his life depended on him being the Prince. And their lives too.

At times he was overcome by loneliness. Being the Prince every unrelenting day, having a family he could not allow to know him. When it became unbearable he would go to the rose garden by himself. Or, now he could ride, head off for the forest. Simply to be by himself, to grieve and breathe freely.

Time alone would make it bearable.

At the end of a year, Rosalie had a baby boy, and when he was six months old they decided they would visit Larken as a family. She said the baby would be fussed over and any changes in Cadd could be put down to marriage and fatherhood. And so it proved. Several relatives remarked at the changes in him, and all said it was for the better. He was so much more pleasant. The King of Larken was especially enamoured of the baby boy.

'Look!' he declared. 'He has two feet.'

Early on, Cadd had made it clear to Lula he had no intention of killing Rosalie's mother. She blustered and tried to seduce him – but he was beyond that, knowing the way she worked. But she did not now have Loo. Even so, he and Rosalie realised she would forever be dangerous. Rosalie was able to put a maid in Lula's household and was given regular reports.

Bild the dwarf was taken from the King and became head of Cadd and Rosalie's household. He was a faithful advisor, true to them both. They came to regard him as a friend, and were proud and honoured to be guests at his wedding.

Of Loo, there was little news for several years. When he escaped he had not gone to Larken but headed for the sea. That was a mistake. At least in Larken he would have had the protection of his family, and they could have hidden him or got him abroad. In a strange port, penniless, Loo was captured by pirates. He was sold on as a galley slave. And for five years he rowed the big sailing ships, chained to his place on the deck. He eventually escaped and made his way back to Larken and to his family. The story he told them was so confused that they prevailed on him to keep silent. For Prince Grude and his wife Princess Rosalie were much loved in Larken and Witland. They had three children – and no one doubted who they were.

But Loo joined up with his cousin, Lady Lula. The King was growing tired of her and had designs on another. Lula saw herself losing any chance of being Queen unless she acted swiftly. With Loo she attempted an assassination of Rosalie's mother. This was foiled by inside information from the maid Rosalie had planted in Lula's household. Loo and Lula were captured and beheaded.

By this time, Cadd was Prince Grude without doubt. Or one doubter, perhaps: Cadd himself. He could wander freely as Prince Grude in either country, and even the country of his birth, now a subject territory of Larken. He did his best to lessen the tributes demanded, prevailing on the King, his father, that unless they wanted constant rebellion they should work with the people, instead of taxing them to starvation. The King was no longer surprised at his son's milder approach, and conceded that it worked as well as his own.

Cadd had his enemies. Princes always do; power attracts them. But he made many friends too. He learnt to be wary, and not always to take people at their word. Deeds mattered more. He had his quarrels with Rosalie. Oh, she was stubborn. She had her father's temper and Cadd found one too. But they always came back together. For they trusted each other, in a world where trust was golden. Perhaps more golden than the love they had.

Or, perhaps the most important part of it, dating from a time when a copy prince had come to woo a princess for his master – and she had won his heart when she bathed his aching stump. While he had seen her vitality and intelligence, and not just her back. A time when both had been prepared to sacrifice their life for the other.

Hell's Chimney
ISBN: 978-0-9536283-7-7

Another fantasy by Derek Smith

In a kingdom enslaved by evil, Toby is running for his life. His stepmother, the Queen, has sent her soldiers after him. Messengers on horseback bear the tale across the land: Prince Toby is a traitor, he killed the King, so he must die.

Hiding in the woods, he finds helpers: a sorry bunch. A young orphaned Lady who has never known work or danger, and a peasant boy who trusts the aristocracy no further than he can spit. How can they bring hope to a country cringing in fear, its hearts and minds as frozen as the winter trees?

Only his father holds the answer. Down in the Underworld, beyond Hell's Chimney, where the dead serve their time. No place for the living. But it's where Toby must go to seek justice.

www.ingramcontent.com/pod-product-compliance
Lightning Source LLC
Chambersburg PA
CBHW051459170626
46811CB00002B/548